FRIEND OF THE DEVIL

ISBN: 978-1-7336429-0-3

Meathouse Publishing
MeathousePublishing@Gmail.com

FRIEND OF THE DEVIL

A NOVEL

JAMES KIRKLAND

meathouse
PUBLISHING
Echo Park

Chapter 1

The gun barrel pressed to my head was cold. It was dark, it was raining, and Bill Walton was singing the Grateful Dead.

Somewhere in the blackness I could hear great sheets of rain falling on the foamy, undulating ocean. The cragged cliff face behind me dropped fifty feet to the beach below, although "beach" makes it sound like it was filled with pleasant golden sand and palm trees. But this was a Puget Sound beach. Its grains of sand were grey rocks the size of a man's fist. Its palm trees were knotted and gnarled pieces of driftwood. And soon the rocks and driftwood would have company: our cold, lifeless bodies.

"In the timbers to Fennario, the wolves are running 'round," Walton sang. His unmistakable voice warbling into the dark. He sung with such gusto, it seemed to tickle our captors. They chuckled. Walton continued, "The winter was so hard and cold, froze ten feet 'neath the ground."

"Hey, Walton, you take requests? How bout 'Box of Rain'?" One of our captors laughed.

Walton ignored them as he continued to sing. "Don't murder me. I beg of you don't murder me." This was too much for the criminals, who fell out laughing. Down on my knees at the edge of a cliff with a gun pointed at my head, I didn't find any of this funny.

"You know what," the leader barked. "Kill Walton last. I want to see how he changes his tune. Shoot the bald one first." That would be me. The bald one. My name is Dave Pasch. I'm a play-by-play announcer for college and NBA basketball. Sometimes I call other sports as well. I'd like to think I'm pretty versatile. And I'm proud to say that I believe I've earned a fair reputation in the broadcasting business. Though it seemed a small satisfaction for me now, staring down the rain-wet barrel of gun.

I scrambled on the sheer walls of my mind for a fingerhold of hope to grab onto. The gun was a Heckler and Koch P-2000. German. Black. Service weapon. Well maintained. I didn't like guns. In fact, for most of my life I hated them. Yet I knew them. I knew them well. All part of the courtship of my wife. You see, my father-in-law, much as he hates the term, is a gun nut. Some folks learn golf to impress their father-in-law. I learned guns. And so I knew the P-2000 jammed less than four times out of a thousand. Not great odds.

There was also a slight chance that our potential murderers could have a change of heart. Very slight. About as slight as Walton doing a broadcast without going off on a tangent about Bobby Weir or the Missoula Floods. No, the gun looked highly functional. Its safety was switched off. Its operator was switched on. They could miss but that would take work. It was literally point blank. The irony. All those years calling sports and now I get shot to death. Then I realized that wasn't ironic. Irony was always hard for me to define, ironically.

Thoughts rushed through my brain as fast as the bullet was about to. My life span could be counted in seconds. How many more breaths did I have left to breathe? Ten? Nine? I took a breath, tried to make it deep. One less now. Eight? It would be soon. That much was for sure. I felt the wind pick up. I was terrified. Bill Walton was smiling.

He appeared to be enjoying the night air. He turned his head to the sky and smiled in his huge toothy grin as the rain rolled down his face. He didn't seem afraid of death of all. In fact, he seemed to welcome it. This bothered me. It's one thing to die. It's another thing to die in the presence of Bill Walton, who was having the time of his life.

I thought back on all the years I'd known Walton. All the times he pissed me off. All those times he ignored me, belittled me, cut me off, wouldn't talk about the damn game. Now this? Shot to death on a cliff on a tiny island in the middle of Puget Sound in the cold dark rain?

Fucking Walton.

"Don't murder me," he belted. "I beg of you don't murder me... pleeease don't murder me."

Our captors roared. It figures. Even on our knees about to be shot, execution style, Walton was more popular than me. "Okay. This is it," we were told. "Any last words?"

I started thinking about what the papers would say when they found our bodies. Then I got mad. I could see the two-inch headline above the fold: Bill Walton this and Bill Walton that. Bill Walton blah, blah, blah. While I, Dave Pasch, play-by-play man of some renown and versatility, held in regard by his peers, reduced to a footnote below the fold. "And the body of play-by-play man Dave Pasch was also found." My life, my memories, my loves, my triumphs, my entire existence would be reduced to a brief, offhand mention somewhere in the fifth paragraph of Walton's long obituary.

That was if they ever found our bodies.

We were about to be dumped in the icy waters of the Puget Sound. A quick snack for orcas or a slow meal for crabs and other nightmarish bottom feeders. This was how I was gonna die?

No. Unacceptable. I cleared my throat. What did I have to lose?

"I have some last words," I said. All eyes turned towards me. This was it. "It's a request actually."

"What is it, bald guy?" the leader growled.

"As the final request of a dying man, please, for the love of God, kill Bill Walton first."

Two days earlier...

Chapter 2

"And it's a one-point game! Washington State with the furious comeback that has Washington stunned! The Huskies were up twenty points just minutes ago and now cling to a one-point lead as they inbound the ball. Washington State scrambling to deny. Pressing full court now. The crowd is on their feet. Hitchcock dribbles up. He's at the top of the key looking to initiate the offense."

"What offense? This is sad!" Walton scoffed.

"Hitchcock looking for the angle for an entry pass. He... finally gets it in to the Huskies big man, Ron Barth. Barth, one dribble, two dribbles, three dribbles... and Barth takes a contested fade-away that's blocked! Washington State center Al Snyder sent that packing!"

"Get that weak stuff outta here, Barth! My goodness, that was soft. You could swaddle a baby with that move! That shot should be used as nesting material for the once endangered California condor! What a great story that is. Back from the brink! What great work they do in the California Condor Center in San Diego."

"Barth is having a tough game but he's young, he's got a great frame on him and has a lot of potential."

"Ron Barth, please!" Walton said. "That soft hook garbage is not going to get it done. This is the big time. This is the Conference of Champions! This is the Pac-12 Championship Tournament! This is the tournament to determine the champion of the Conference of Champions."

"And during that rant, Bill, Washington State scored a very exciting basket to go up one with twelve seconds left," I said as the horn sounded. "And Washington calls their final timeout to set up what they hope will be the game-winning shot."

We heard the voice of our new producer, Stephanie Walker, crackle in our headphones. "Hey guys, we're not cutting to commercial, talk us through the timeout."

I was still getting used to having a different voice in my ear. Stephanie started as our producer just a couple weeks ago. I don't think Bill had even started to process it. For all I know, he might not have even noticed that we had a new producer. This was our third game with Stephanie and things had gone relatively smoothly. But our first two games were not close in the final minutes. Broadcasters and their producers are not immune to the tension and pressure of big games and big moments.

"Twelve seconds left. Washington has the ball. Who takes the shot, Bill?"

Stephanie's voice came back in our ears. "Dante Hitchcock has an effective field goal percentage of .552, which is 17.3 percent better than anyone else on the team."

"Somebody's telling me some numbers in my ear and I don't know what they are talking about," Walton said obtusely.

"I think, Bill, that we just hear our producer giving us some data. Hitchcock has an effective field goal percentage of .552, which is seventeen percent better than anyone else on the roster."

"I don't know what you just said. Sounds like poetry written by a calculator."

I winced. As a broadcasting team, we just committed a costly turnover. And Stephanie and Walton were both to blame. Stephanie hadn't yet learned that Walton couldn't handle a bunch of numbers being poured into his ear. Stats and modern analytics did nothing but confuse and anger Walton. It was like putting a mirror in front of a snake. Maybe he understood the numbers very well and he just didn't care for them. Maybe he pretended to not understand. That seemed just as likely.

Walton compounded the situation, of course, by calling it out. That made it several times worse. Mistakes are made in live broadcast television. They happen. The role of the professional broadcaster is to absorb them, digest them, and make sure that the audience sitting at home, or at a sports bar, never catches a whiff that anything but a perfect broadcast ever happened. I tried my best to absorb the clumsy jab at an unseen producer who the audience had never heard of.

"It's actually interesting data, Bill. Given to us by Stephanie Walker, who's doing a great job stepping in after our long-term producer, the legendary Bob Smithsonian, retired after a glorious forty-year career to chase fish around the Florida Keys. Good luck, Bob, and of course, welcome, Stephanie."

"Bob! What a producer! Come back, Bob! Unretire! We miss you!" Walton must have sensed the daggers I was staring into him because he finally shut up. The ref whistled. The crowd yelled. The inbounder slapped the ball.

"Here we go. Wallace inbounds to Hitchcock. It looks like Hitchcock is trying to get it to Barth in the post."

"Of course, he's got four inches on his counterpart, please!" Walton bemoaned. "They need to feed him the ball and he needs to throw it down! Establish his will on the block! Call in the strength of the mighty island of his homeland. The Maori people! The native people of New Zealand! Unconquered for thousands of years! You know if he keeps playing this soft, they might not let him back in! Passport revoked. They play rugby down there, that is a brutally violent sport."

"It looks like Barth has drifted over to the corner."

"Post up, man! What are you doing? He's floating out to the three-point line like a cloud!"

"Washington State playing some very tight defense as the referees have swallowed their whistles. Clock down to four seconds! Hitchcock abandons the play. Dribbles to the top of the key. Running out of time. Hitchcock takes a wild, contested three as time runs out…" The buzzer sounded. "And it's good! Washington eliminates their in-state rival in a thriller! And listen to this Seattle crowd!"

"Okay. Guys." Stephanie, again in our headsets. "We just have to do the last billboard and we're outta here. So, coming up, it's the Franklin's Insurance Dunk of the Game. Going with Hitchcock from the first half. And, go." Bill covered his microphone with his hand. Refusing, as always, to use the cough button conveniently located under his other hand. "Gonna get some water," Bill whispered to me. And he started to take a long pull from his BPA-free Nalgene bottle. I gritted my teeth and begged God for patience.

"Who do you think is the going to be the Franklin Insurance Dunk of the Game, Bill?" Now it was Bill's turn to look annoyed.

"Gee, Dave, I really don't know. Did anyone dunk in this game?"

"Yes, they did, Bill. There were several dunks."

"Dave, when I was learning the game in high school and college, the dunk shot was illegal. And it made me a better basketball player. Sometimes I think we should go back to those days to help young players develop the skills they desperately need."

"So you're saying you don't have a choice for the Franklin Insurance Dunk of the Game?"

"All I saw is dunks that could have been. The dunks that never were! Barth! Dunk now or forever hold your peace."

"Well, Dante Hitchcock with this nasty tomahawk slam in the first half is our Franklin Insurance Dunk of the Game. And that's it for us, here in Seattle. The Washington Huskies get the win and thrill half of the hometown crowd by moving on in the Pac-12 Tournament. For Bill Walton, I'm Dave Pasch. Back to you in the studio." I took my headset off and rubbed my temples.

"I think that went great," Walton said, smiling. "Nice work, Dave." I honestly couldn't tell if he was being sarcastic or not. He offered a fist bump I pretended not to notice. Walton checked his phone. On the back was a sticker of the scraggly visage of Jerry Garcia. To me he always looked like a Muppet grandfather. I didn't get it. The band. The music. It just wasn't for me. I stood and stretched.

The Pac-12 Tournament this year was at Key Arena in Seattle. A nice place, but the former home of Supersonics was a shadow of its former glory. The NBA had moved on. Now, in the rainy winters of the Northwest, after the Seahawks season is over, with the Mariners not making the playoffs for the twentieth straight year, the basketball-starved hoop fans from the 206 area code turned their longing gaze to the college game. The Dawgs of Washington had a good team this year. Putting together a late season run after a rocky start, positioning themselves firmly on the bubble. A strong showing here could punch their ticket to the big tournament. The dance.

It was a great game but, as a broadcast team, we had an awful telecast. Fortunately, it was a late game and the bosses back east were asleep. Stephanie, green as she was, probably didn't know that. I saw her come out of the tunnel and walk up the length of the hardwood floor. Stephanie was in her thirties, black, and on the shorter side, but carried herself with the confidence and swagger of a much taller person. She was walking fast, her ponytail bouncing. She pulled her purple binder of show notes out of the well-worn tan backpack that was her constant companion. We had been on polite "getting to know you" terms her first two weeks. I anticipated that to continue.

She slammed her purple binder on our table. I guess not.

"Bill, with all due respect, what the hell was that?"

"Stephanie, please," Walton started, folding his arms in his go-to posture of standoffishness. Stephanie mirrored him.

"No. Please, nothing. First, you call me out on air, which I didn't like, but I can handle. But you cannot. Stress on the word cannot. Cannot screw up the billboards. That is the one thing you cannot do. You do get what the billboards are, don't you, Bill? Why we call them bills, Bill? Because they pay the bills. They pay for all of this. They pay your salary. They pay my salary. They pay Pasch's salary."

"Couch cushions could pay Pasch's salary!"

What an insanely cheap shot. Bill was in rare form tonight.

"You're messing with the money, Walton. And you're not listening to me," Stephanie said.

"It's not that I'm not listening to you, I just can't hear stats. Tell Pasch the numbers. I'm the color guy. I'm Picasso! I paint in words! Guernica!"

"Okay. All right. Cool. You're testing me. I get it. But I need to let you know right now, Bill, I do not accept these tests. Yes, I'm new, but I wasn't born yesterday. I won't be treated this way. Would you have treated Bob Smithsonian that way?"

"Never!" Walton said. "Because Bob left us alone! He was a great producer because he stayed out of my way and let me do my thing."

"Oh yeah, Bill? Did John Wooden just 'stay out of your way'? Did Dr. Jack Ramsay just 'let you do your own thing'? Is the problem not that I'm telling you what to do but that I'm a woman telling you what to do?"

"Lady, you are barking up the wrong tree. I am a militant feminist! I rode the crest of the Second Wave with my dear friends Gloria Steinem and Betty Friedan. We laid down our bodies so that women would have the right to control their own."

"Bill, I wasn't asking for receipts on your woke credentials," she deadpanned.

"This is who I am and who I've always been! Check my bona-fides! Ask Joan Baez! In fact, you could call her right—"

"Let's get something straight, "she cut Walton off. I was impressed, took me years to learn how to do that. "You can go on your rants. You can talk about your hippie nonsense. All that's fine. I get it. But there's gonna be numbers. There's gonna be narratives. And there is most definitely gonna be billboards, Bill. That's my job." She held eye contact with Bill until he looked away. I cleared my throat.

"Bill. Stephanie. It was a great game. Or a fine game. It was a game. Anyway, we got through it. Let's all have some patience. It's gonna take a while to get used to each other. But we'll get there. Together. Right?" The tension hung in the air like a half-court shot at the buzzer. Finally, Stephanie nodded.

"All right, let's start again fresh tomorrow. Tonight doesn't matter. Bosses back east are asleep anyway." She walked away and I smirked. Maybe there was more to our new producer than I thought.

Chapter 3

It's true in concerts and true in theater and true in basketball: when the show is good, people don't want to leave. They linger. Basking in the afterglow. "Soaking in the vibes," as Walton would put it. A win for the Huskies against their in-state rivals in the conference tournament? That was some pretty good vibes.

Fans were meandering. Slowly making their way to the exits. I pulled out my phone. I wasn't in a hurry either. I scrolled the usual apps. Waiting for the crowd to thin. My Twitter feed was abuzz with people talking about the game and, of course, talking about Walton. They were mostly positive, some confused, a few hated the unprofessionalism he displayed. Most laughed. No mentions of me, other than one random guy, @bearcatsguy77, speculating how much I must hate working with Walton. I laughed to myself. Thank you, @bearcatsguy77.

My phone vibrated. My wife. I unspooled my earbuds and answered.

"Did you see the game?" I asked.

"Oh my God."

"So you saw it."

"He's unhinged."

"I know. But that's why people tune in, right?"

"Hey. People love you. Remember that."

"I know. I know." But I didn't know. Did they love me or did they just love him? Was he the lion at the circus everyone came to see and I was just some stiff in a top hat holding a chair? My wife, somewhat of a mind reader, must have picked up on the pitch in my voice.

"Honey, I think you are a hero every time you don't punch him in the face." I laughed. She had a way of relaxing me. One of the reasons I loved her. One of the many.

"I miss you. Give the kids my love. I'll be home in a few days."

Then my wife and I said how much we love each other, which we try to do as often as we can every single day. I hung up the phone and glanced over and saw Walton. He was having an animated discussion with a tall, striking, salt-and-pepper-haired man who was well-dressed in a very Seattle way. REI pants. Arc'teryx jacket. Patagonia pullover with a dress shirt underneath. It was to the Pacific Northwest what the bespoke three-piece Italian suit was to Wall Street. I could tell, just by looking at him, this man was successful. I could also tell something was wrong. He was upset.

All my life I've had a highly developed sense of curiosity. A strong pull to the unknown like gravity towards a black hole. A tractor beam towards the mysteries of life, that, once activated, was very hard to turn off. I was much like the proverbial cat, only with significantly fewer proverbial lives. Curiosity is my defining trait. And I was curious to know who this rich guy talking to Walton was and what they were talking about. Looking back, maybe I should have minded my own business. But I didn't. Damned curiosity. Another cat bites the dust. I walked over.

Walton introduced the man, who turned out to be one of his old UCLA teammates, Phil Engels. "An old friend and a great guy. He's a pharmacist."

"I'm in pharmaceuticals, Bill."

"That's what I said!"

I tried to shake hands with Phil, but he didn't notice. It was clear something was wrong. He said he couldn't talk with other people around so we brought him to our dressing room.

The linoleum floor and fluorescent ceiling lights made the innards of the arena feel surprisingly school-like. We walked past framed pictures documenting Key Arena's past glories. Pictures of Shawn Kemp, Gary Payton, and other members of the legendary 90s Supersonics. Various musical luminaries that performed here. Lucky for me, they were labeled. Prince, Bruce Springsteen, Nirvana, Macklemore, and Pearl Jam. Eddie Vedder sweating like a pig, screaming into a microphone. Disgusting. We turned a corner and ran into the referees from tonight's game, looking very different from their in-game personas. Their black and white vertical striped shirts were untucked. One was drinking something out of a brown paper bag, another had an unlit cigarette in his mouth. No matter how well or poorly they had performed, Walton always took a moment to insult the referees after a game. It was a little tradition of his, I assume carried over from his playing days, that I never agreed with. The referees worked hard, traveled constantly, didn't get paid nearly as much as they deserved, and got nothing but abuse from players, coaches, and fans. Yet Walton never passed up an opportunity to put them down.

"Hey guys, I just wanted to let you know that was one of the worst officiated games I have ever seen. Terrible from start to finish."

Verne Harris, a wonderful gentleman who's been admirably officiating games for over thirty years, had a quick reply: "Eat shit, Walton." Bill smirked as he walked on.

Our dressing room was small and cramped. On the far wall stood a clothing rack where we hung our street clothes. I had an overcoat to put on over my suit. I always liked to look respectable. On camera and off. Walton had a tie-dye shirt. He was already wearing a tie-dye shirt that he was given before the game. It was the official shirt of the Pac-12 Tourney, tie-dyed rainbow blue. So he just put the other tie-dye shirt on top. Layering the tie-dye. The left side of the room was walled with vanity mirrors framed by Hollywood-style sixty-watt bulbs. More than a few were burnt out. It didn't take long to notice that this was not an NBA stadium anymore. Not for a long time. A waist-high shelf beneath the mirrors was cluttered with water bottles, coffee mugs, plastic forks and knives, napkins, and a few unopened fortune cookies. The bagless garbage can was full of food containers, remnants of our dinner. Thai. The room smelled like peanut sauce and Old Spice. The Old Spice was mine. Walton used a natural blend of essential oils that, in my experience sitting next to the man for almost a decade, did nothing but accelerate the sweating process.

A couple chairs were scattered about. I offered one to Phil and Walton folded himself down on another.

"Okay, Phil," Walton said. "What's going on?"

He hesitated. "I don't know Bill. I think it's a good idea for me to keep this quiet as possible. Dave, no offense but I don't know you. I've known Bill forty-five years."

"Phil, please," Walton said. "Anything you can tell me, you can say to Dave. I trust him." Walton caught my eye and winked. I wasn't sure what to make of this. I had never heard Walton speak like this before and I couldn't remember him ever winking at me. He wanted me to stay. And I wasn't sure why. The situation seemed serious. My heart started to beat faster. Walton beckoned Phil to continue.

"Well. Thing is. Um. My daughter, Abigail..." He paused. Took a breath.

"Abigail is my goddaughter," Walton explained. "Phil and his wife Helen's only child. Freshman right here at UW." Phil nodded. He was searching his pockets for something. Like a drunk man looking for his keys. He sniffed and I realized he was looking for a tissue. The poor guy could barely speak. Walton went on. "She's a wonderful girl. And is growing into a wonderful woman. So full of life. So kind. So funny. She's studying design, right, Phil?"

Phil broke then. Full sobs. Breath coming in choppy and phlegmy. He tried to clear his throat. Walton handed him a bottle of water. He screwed off the top and drank. His hands were shaking. His eyes wet.

"Bill, she's been kidnapped."

Chapter 4

"What?" Walton exclaimed. "You're kidding! Who took her?"

"I don't know. I don't fucking know!" He collapsed then. Into himself, into the chair. I looked for a tissue. The box was empty. Walton reached out his long arm and held his friend's hand. I found some unused napkins in a drawer and handed them to him. He took a moment to blow his nose and regain his composure.

"Phil. Just breathe. Tell us what happened," I asked.

"This morning she texted me a video. Well, it was from her phone. I assumed it was from her. I don't want to watch this again, but you have to see this."

Phil then played us the video. It was a close-up of Abigail's face, in a dark room, with two machine guns pointed at her head. She was screaming, "Pay them, daddy! Pay them!" Phil winced at the words he must have already heard many times that day. Then a creepy robot voice came on, it sounded like Siri, and said, "Mr. Engels, you have three days to put together ten million dollars in untraceable, unmarked, nonsequential cash. Ten million dollars is the price of your daughter's life."

"My God," I said.

As Abigail continued to cry, the creepy robot voice told Phil they would kill his daughter if he went to the police or FBI. The video ended with one last horrific scream from Abigail and the screen went black. The sound of the fluorescent lights buzzing over our heads was as loud as a passing airplane. Phil finally broke the silence.

"I've tried to call her back. I sent a million texts. Nothing. No response."

"Did you try using Find My Phone?"

"Yes. I tried. I kept trying. It can't find her phone. They must have her phone off or they're underground or in a cave!"

Phil broke down in tears. Walton comforted him, wrapping a long arm around his friend's shaking shoulders.

"Well," I said, "I think we have to go to the cops."

"They said they'd kill her if I went to the cops!" Phil barked.

"Yeah," I replied calmly. "But that's probably just an empty threat, right?"

"We can't take that chance," Walton answered firmly. "No cops. We're not going to risk calling that bluff."

"Okay then," I said, quickly wrapping my brain around the situation. "If we don't call the cops, then we do what the cops would tell us to do: Pay the money and get your daughter back."

I asked Phil if he could put together ten million dollars in three days and he told me it was already on its way. "I had to move some things around but I don't care. Obviously. I just want Abigail back. I'll pay anything."

"Okay then," Walton said in his most calming voice. "You've done everything you can. All they want is money. Everything will be fine."

"Thank you, Bill. Thanks." Phil nodded. "I should go home to Helen. I just… I had to talk to somebody. And I knew Bill was in town. I'm sorry. It's okay. It's okay. I'll just pay the money and everything will be fine."

Phil stumbled up and grabbed his coat. We said goodbyes and told him we'd be in touch tomorrow. Before I closed the door, I hesitated and asked Phil, "Just out of curiosity. When was the last time you spoke to Abigail?"

Phil stopped, thinking. "Last night. We texted. She was going to the library with her roommate, Kaitlin. I told her I loved her and… and..." He turned away from us as he started crying again. I watched the poor guy stumble down the linoleum hallway.

I closed the door and turned to Walton, who fell into a chair, drained by the weight of what we had just heard. I hated to make things worse, but I told him what I was thinking.

"Bill, did you know that eighty percent of kidnappings result in the victim being killed?"

"No, Dave, I did not know that."

"My wife, she loves true crime documentaries. It's all she'll watch. We watched one on kidnapping a few months ago. What happens is that eight out of ten times the kidnappers will slip up. Say a name. The victim catches a glimpse of a face. Kidnappers are rarely criminal masterminds, more often desperate amateurs with nothing to lose. And after they mess up, they wind up taking the money and leaving a corpse."

Walton was quiet. He looked off into the middle distance. He stood up.

"Well then, Dave, we have to find her before something happens."

"What? No," I stammered. "Us? Find her? We can't get involved."

"We have to get involved, Dave. And deep down, you know we do. That's why you asked Phil about the last time he heard from Abigail."

"No, Bill, I was just… the question just popped into my mind."

"Dave, think about it. Phil's a mess. We can't go to the cops or the FBI. And right now Abigail is out there, somewhere, with guns pointed at her head. We're her last best chance at staying alive."

"Bill, you can't really be seriously thinking about…" Walton didn't smile.

"We're going to find her, Dave. And we're going to get her back. And we're going to start right now."

Chapter 5

The dorm was empty. It was a Friday night and the campus was jumping. Most people were out partying. As college kids are wont to do. We followed the security guard through the labyrinth of the dorm. We passed doors with dry erase boards filled with messages and drawings, some appropriate, most not. The guard was a large black man named Grant, who looked like he spent most of his life sitting down. He told us, for the fifth time, that he would normally never do anything like this. But, luckily for us, he was a huge Bill Walton fan and he led us to Abigail and Kaitlin's room on the second floor. We arrived at the door and knocked.

"Coming!" We heard from inside the door. Then it opened. Abigail's roommate, Kaitlin, was one of the few students who decided to stay in for the night.

"Kaitlin, my name is Dave Pasch, this is Bill Walton."

"Hi," she said, confused.

"We're friends of your roommate Abigail's father and we really need to talk to you."

"Oh, sure, come on in. Sorry for the mess. I wasn't expecting… old strangers at 11:30 at night." I stepped inside. Bill took a quick selfie with a delighted Grant and followed me into the room.

Kaitlin looked like the type of kid who believed what her parents and teachers told her, 'til recently. Maybe a friend let her borrow Howard Zinn's *The People's History of the United States* or maybe she watched a few YouTube documentaries and the algorithms sent her down a few too many rabbit holes that she hadn't yet navigated her way out of. She wore her hair in long blonde dreadlocks that were well maintained. Large bangles around her wrists. Necklaces entwined with various crystals swung from her neck. An assortment of rings bedazzled her fingers. She was pretty in an old soul, young face sort of way. She was in a torn Earth First T-shirt featuring a balled-up fist in front of a picture of the globe. Her eyes were the color of well-worn blue jeans.

"What's this all about? Is everything okay?"

"Kaitlin, we need to talk to you about the last time you saw Abigail. We know you went to the library together last night."

Walton could immediately tell by the look on her face that they did not go to the library last night. "Kaitlin, it's okay," he told her. "I wouldn't trust a kid who told their parents the truth all the time. We're not here to bust you for living your life. We just need to know where you and Abigail went last night."

"Okay, yeah, we went to a bar and hung out for a while, then she ghosted me. I haven't seen—" Kaitlin suddenly realized why two strange men had come to her room at 11:30 at night asking questions about her roommate. "Oh God. What's going on? Is Abi okay?"

"This is going to be hard for you to hear," I said. "But Abigail has been kidnapped. And please don't tell anyone we told you that."

"Oh my God." Her eyes went wide. She covered her mouth with one hand, while the other grabbed an old quilt on her bed and pulled it to her chest.

"We need your help, Kaitlin. We want to get her back, safe. To do that, we need to figure out who did this. As quickly and quietly as possible. Tell us what happened last night," I asked.

"We went to the Smokeshow. It's a bar on University Way. We got there about 11:00. We were having a good time and then she disappeared about 1:30?" Kaitlin checked her phone. "Yeah, I texted her at 1:47 asking where she was. I stuck around until they closed at 2:00. Then I came back here. Oh God. I thought she just met some guy and took off. She does it all the time. I mean, don't tell her dad that. But I didn't see her leave. She was just there one second and gone the next."

"Okay, back up. How did you get into a bar? You're freshmen. Underage."

"Come on, Pasch, they have fake IDs," Walton boomed. "She's old enough to vote, die for her country, but not have a beer? It's ridiculous! And what does that have to do with anything?! Please."

I was furious. Walton never missed an opportunity to berate me. On and off camera. I was just asking questions that came to my mind. I'm not a detective.

"Actually, we don't have fake IDs."

"Then how did you get in?" I asked.

"The Smokeshow has this one bouncer who, like, when he's working... he does this thing, where..." She shifted, nervous.

"Kaitlin, every bit of information we get can be important."

She took a breath and continued. "Okay, yeah… he'll let… he has a thing where, if you show your… you know, like flash… he'll let you in."

Bill curled up his long fingers into a huge pale fist. His extraordinary thumb wrapping around the four fingers like a halter around four horses. His bony wrist a chariot.

"What is this man's name?" Walton asked slowly.

"Cal."

"And what does Cal look like?"

"Um, he's kinda really… stocky. Not that tall. White guy. Short and wide."

Walton headed for the door. "Come on, Dave, let's go have a conversation with this Cal."

"Be careful, Mr. Walton, Cal can be pretty rough. He used to play football."

"Football player, huh? Let's go see how tough he is without the helmet and pads. And Kaitlin, next time you want to go to a bar, use a fake ID."

Chapter 6

Walton was walking faster than usual. His lanky gait held a limp that varied from slight to severe depending on the weather conditions, derived from the numerous lower leg and foot injuries he suffered during his playing days. As Walton said, his body was like a VW bus with a million miles and not a lot of original parts. Sometimes it took a while to start, but it always did, it always ran.

We hurried to my rental car parked in the red zone next to the dorm. It had a parking ticket from the campus police, which, I learned long ago, I could completely ignore. Walton had his own rental. Which he never used. There were times I did feel like somewhere along the way I had become Bill's play-by-play man and personal chauffeur. The funny thing was, I didn't mind. I'd never admit this to Walton, but I liked driving. No. That's not true. I loved driving.

"How are you doing, Bill?" I asked. "You good?" I started the car and backed out of the spot.

Walton cracked his acorn-sized knuckles. It sounded like several cars backfiring. "I'm not good. How can these people do this to these girls? They're children, for God's sake. This bouncer has a world of hurt coming his way. Oh my goodness, he has no idea."

I steered into traffic and navigated to the bar. Google Maps indicated it was not far off campus. A five-minute drive up and down the city's hills, ending on University Way, a bustling street with electrical bus lines strung down the middle.

I knew by the sound of the wipers squeaking across the windshield that the rain had finally stopped. Paused would be a better word. It never fully stops, not in spring in Seattle. I steered the rental car with my left hand and stopped the wipers with my right.

The rental car, a full-size Chrysler 300, was a nice change for me. It was black and sleek. Far more muscle than my hybrid back home. I liked having a few extra ponies under the hood, especially with the network buying the gas. I goosed it down an empty street just to feel the rush. The energy.

We found the bar. It was easy. Bright neon sign next to plastic posters sponsored by big beer brands advertising different drink promotions. I parked up the street and we walked over, passing a couple kids huddled up, exhaling giant clouds of smoke after inhaling from a small rectangular instrument.

"Vaping." Walton shook his head. "Call me crazy, Pasch, but I'll pass on the digital water vapor. Give me the old-fashioned analog smoke. Combustion!"

We arrived at the Smokeshow. There was a line to get in, kids showing their IDs to the bouncer, who had to be Cal. He was a greasy, stout man, no stranger to the gym or the late-night burger stand. He looked like an ex-football player, definitely a lineman. Probably a center or a guard. Low to the ground. I supposed as a bouncer the only job requirements are being hard to knock down and hard to get around. He looked like he qualified for both.

Walton cut the line, walking straight to him, but the bouncer didn't notice; he was busy ogling the coeds as they staggered out into the street.

"You Cal?" Bill asked.

Cal smiled at a pack of girls who looked like a high school cheerleading squad. He had two huge front teeth. Those teeth, and the shape of his body, made him look like a human beaver. He finally peeled his lecherous eyes away from the girls. He took his time turning his head and came face to navel with Bill Walton.

In any other company Cal would seem intimidating. But he wasn't in any other company. He was in Bill Walton's company. Walton was always listed at 6'11" because, when he was nineteen years old, John Wooden simply declared him to be that height. Shorting him at least an inch or so. I suppose so other teams would underestimate him. And to this day Walton refuses to be called a seven-footer. He loves the idea of having been a scrappy underdog to the likes of Jabbar, Olajuwon, and Ewing. But, trust me, the man is seven feet tall. Easily. He might even be taller but it's hard to tell. He always slouches. But he wasn't slouching now. Walton was standing as tall as I'd ever seen him. I wish I had a ruler.

"Who's asking, big man?"

"My name is Bill Walton and I have some questions to ask you." Walton never broke eye contact. "Now, Cal, it is very important you answer my questions honestly and to the best of your knowledge." Cal took a step back. He sized up Walton. And kept sizing him up. And up

"You remember seeing these girls last night?" He gestured at me. I took out a Polaroid I had borrowed from Kaitlin's corkboard.

One of her and Abigail. The day they had moved in together, smiling, arms wrapped around each other. Cal glanced at it. He shrugged.

"Eh. I don't remember, lots of people come here. I don't pay attention to every girl who comes in and out of here."

"Not from what I've seen," I said.

"What?" Cal sneered.

"It seems like you've paid a lot of attention to the young girls who come in and out of here," I said, growing in bravado. Standing up to bullies, I'll admit, is much easier when you're standing next to Bill Walton. Cal turned and looked at me. He tried to regain his intimidation factor. It didn't work. I stared right back. His eyes began to dart here and there like an animal cornered. I didn't like it. Wild animals are the most dangerous when cornered. I assumed it worked the same with wild bouncers.

"I know you let her in. What we want to know is, did you see her leave?" Walton asked.

"I told you I don't remember, lots of people come in and out of here." His tone of voice sharpened. He wanted this conversation to be over, stat.

"You need a cup of coffee to clear your memory? Let's go get a cup of coffee," Walton said, grabbing Cal by the arm. Cal shrugged him off. He was quicker than he looked.

"I don't need a cup of coffee," said Cal. "I need you to get up out of my face."

"Not until you answer my question." Cal didn't move. A small crowd had gathered. Some college kids started to recognize Walton. Others just felt the vibe of conflict and were drawn in. Primal response. The schoolyard rush to see a fight on the playground. Like a moth drawn to fire. A chucklehead in the crowd egged Cal on.

"Hey, Cal, you gonna let Bill Walton punk you like that?" The crowd let out a few intoxicated laughs.

"Do you remember letting some underage girls in your bar last night, Cal? Do you remember breaking the law?" Cal was getting flushed. Redness started to creep into his face.

"You know what, I don't know who the fuck you are, old dude, but I'm starting to really not like you. So last warning. Get the fuck out of here before I fuck you up." The crowd let out an "oooh" at that one.

"You don't want to do this, Cal. Let's just have a conversation." Walton was nearly pleading now. "I beg you to reconsider. You have a choice here."

"Yeah. You know what? You're right."

Cal stepped back, reached into his jacket, and took out what looked like a tiny fire extinguisher. But after he yanked off the red tab and pulled the trigger, I saw the tiny fire extinguisher was a giant can of pepper spray.

I felt it immediately. My throat closed like someone was choking me. My ears, my nose, my mouth felt like they were on fire. It felt like I was swimming in a pool of hot sauce with no goggles. I tried to hold my ground but my legs involuntarily carried me away. I turned around after a few paces. The rest of the crowd had, like me, made a swift and frightened retreat. College kids ran like chickens sans heads. Most of them were coughing and spitting and the rest were running and screaming. I used my sleeve to wipe my tears and tried to ignore the pain.

Through my tears I saw him. Walton. As calm as you'd like, in a cloud of pepper spray. Cal aimed for his head and Walton blocked the stream of pepper spray with the palm of his right hand. Then he stepped forward, using all seven feet of his reach to swipe at the can with his left. Cal parried and kept spraying. They wrestled for control. The can hissed. Some of the spray went straight up. Some to the left, the right. Collateral damage. It sent a cloud of pepper into the street. Flocks of fleeing bar patrons screaming. All felt the sting.

The can started to cough and hesitate. It slowed to a trickle and stopped. It dropped from his hand and clinked to the asphalt like an empty beer can thrown from a passing car. Cal broke away from Walton, blinking hard. He was playing it off, but he was feeling it. How could he not? In that noxious liquid lived the souls of a million angry bees. Finally, the pepper spray cloud parted. Walton hadn't moved. He was crying. For sure. Great rivers of tears fell freely from his puffy, red eyes. His mouth was buttoned closed. When the spray cleared, he inhaled mightily. Was he holding his breath the whole time? He cleared his throat.

"Please, Cal, it doesn't have to be this way." But apparently it did. Desperate, Cal threw a wild haymaker that Walton caught easily in midair. Walton's huge hand enveloped the bouncer's fist like a solar eclipse. Totality. Walton could have ended it then, but Cal stopped struggling. I saw a flash of buck teeth. He was smirking.

That's when I saw the other bouncer. He wore a black leather jacket and gripped a Louisville Slugger. He was creeping behind Walton. I tried to warn him, but the pepper spray had closed my throat like an invisible noose. Words came out as coughs.

"Now, Cal, let's all just calm down. Just answer the question..." Walton was saying.

He didn't see the second bouncer, another ex-football type. If Cal was a lineman, here came the outside linebacker. Taller. More athletic. He took small steps. Stealthy. Coiled. Lining up his swing. I tried to yell again. Loud coughs. He twisted his body to swing, his leather jacket creaking as he did. That sound was all Walton needed. He was already moving. The mechanism was activated. The machinery of his body was working on old code, well-used muscle memory. The footwork, even in Walton's advanced years, was perfect. Drop step, pivot, elbows high. I swear he even looked like he was holding an unseen basketball in his hands. His right leg pushed off and sent the upper body, complete with elbow at the ready and twisted left. The linebacker and his baseball bat were at the apex of the backswing when the large and pointy elbow caught him cleanly on his jaw. Ouchy. Walton kept his elbows high and watched as the linebacker crumbled to the street. Out. Cold. Cal stopped grinning. Then he ran. As fast as his little legs would allow. Long jacket flapping like a beaver tail.

Walton ambled towards me. His eyes were crimson. His face Niagara. I handed him my handkerchief.

"Thank you," he said, calm as a clam.

"Bill," I said. "Bill, you..." I wheezed. I had to pause to cough and spit. My eyes were still on fire.

"What?"

"You took a full can of pepper spray directly into your face! Everyone else is out here puking on the street and you barely flinched. How is that possible?!"

"Dave, it was 1973, my friends were dying in South Vietnam. Our country was committing atrocities. The least I could do was spend a summer building an immunity to tear gas and pepper spray."

I tried to respond but only hacked a cough. Somehow, even with the pepper spray disappearing from the air, my eyes were feeling worse.

"Sh— should we… g-g-go to the hospital?"

Walton slapped me on the back. "Come on, Dave. Let's get a drink."

Chapter 7

The milk Walton ordered for us soothed my throat like aloe on a sunburn. "It's the only thing that helps," Walton said as he ordered another round of "Moo Juice."

The bar was empty. Most people cleared out when the pepper spray went off. Even inside you could still feel the bite in the air. The bartender looked like a vampire in black eye makeup and an eyebrow ring. That's all I could see because she had her T-shirt pulled up over her nose and mouth. She was serving the last few customers whose need for alcohol clearly outweighed their need for fresh air. I looked around and noticed a few security cameras around the room. That was good news.

I pointed the cameras out to Bill. He nodded, took a deep sip of his milk, and poured the rest on top of his head so it fell down into his eyes. The milk dripped off Walton's face to the floor. The bartender stared at Walton. Walton stared back.

"We'd like to speak to your manager."

The vampire lady pointed to a room in the back marked EMPLOYEES ONLY.

We walked over and Walton threw open the door to a small office with a small desk and a small man. He had a receding hairline and a bad goatee. Not that there are any good goatees, but this one was particularly bad. His name was Ryan and he had a nervous vibe. His right leg bopped up and down like a piston at a red light. Ryan was jumpy. Maybe it was because an angry Bill Walton stood above him drenched in milk.

"Ryan, when Bobby Weir first met Jerry Garcia in a Palo Alto music store, New Year's Eve 1964, he liked him right away," Walton said. "I feel the opposite about meeting you. Ryan, I don't like you. I don't like you at all. And we are not going to start a band tonight. And we are not going to be friends. But you are going to jam on that video machine so we can watch the security footage from last night. Right, Ryan?"

Ryan nodded, a bit shell-shocked. "Who are you?"

"Doesn't matter who we are, we need to see the security footage for the entrance of the club outside starting at 11:00 last night."

The small man surrendered. With a few clicks Ryan found the footage. He sucked on a can of Red Bull while we watched a few minutes of the footage. Packs of young people filing up to the door and going inside.

"Stop," Walton said. "There they are."

Ryan hit a button and the footage snapped back into real time. Indeed. It was them. Abigail with her brown hair and a green top. Kaitlin, blonde dreadlocks bouncing, in a hippie top and lots of jewelry. The two girls walked up to Cal, who stood at the entrance of the bar.

"Watch this," Walton said. Then he turned to the nervous man in the office chair. "Because two underage girls are about to enter your bar."

"What? No way. Cal is supposed to be checking IDs."

"Well, that's not all he's checking," I explained. "That creep is making underage girls lift their shirts to get in." Walton went to cover the screen with his hands, but the girls faced away from the camera. It was still clear what they were doing and, by his reaction, it was also clear that Ryan didn't know.

"No. Oh, no," Ryan stammered. "I had no idea he was letting in minors. That's stupid. He could get us shut down."

"Yeah," I added. "And it's also wrong."

"Right. Totally wrong. I'm gonna fire his ass."

"Both of them," Walton said. "You're gonna need new bouncers, pal."

Ryan nodded. He tried to drink from the Red Bull can, but it was empty. He shook it and tried to toss the can in his little wastebasket. He missed. Badly. He wiped his brow. This was the sweat of the frightened. The smell of the sweat caused by fear is more potent in a small room and you didn't need to be a dog to smell it.

"Keep going," Walton said. "They went inside, switch to the cameras in there." Ryan hit another button and we watched as the girls entered and smushed together for what looked like a celebratory selfie. They headed to the bar and Ryan switched to that camera, but we couldn't really see them. The camera was a side view of just the bartenders. The vampire was there, with a few others, scrambling to serve beers and the cheap, colorful drinks enjoyed by people who want to get drunk without tasting alcohol.

"Can you switch to another camera that faces the girls?" I asked.

"No," Ryan explained. "The cameras there are focused on the bartenders. I'm more worried about my staff stealing from me than I am about whatever a bunch of drunk idiots might be up to." As if on cue, we saw Kaitlin's arms reach into frame, with her recognizable hemp bracelets. The bartender handed her two giant green drinks and pocketed the cash while pretending to put the money in the till. Ryan squealed, "Son of a bitch, you see that?! Now I need a new bartender too!"

"Never mind your staffing concerns," Walton chided him while pointing at the screen with a giant, king crab-sized finger. "They went over there, go to that camera."

A couple more clicks and we saw Abigail and Kaitlin at the jukebox where they were approached by a couple of guys. Frat boy types. They talked, they flirted, they drank. Typical college bar activities. It all seemed quite harmless.

Walton had Ryan fast-forward through the footage. We saw Abigail and Kaitlin dance with the boys in fast motion, looking a bit like an old film of Babe Ruth rounding the bases.

"Stop!"

A guy stormed up to Abigail. He was big, broad-shouldered. Someone she recognized. Spiky hair. Lots of gel. He was upset. They argued. The frat boys stepped in and they all started shoving. As things escalated, Cal and the linebacker arrived. All fingers pointed to Spiky Hair and they dragged him away while he shouted and pointed at Abigail. After he was gone, Kaitlin and Abigail split away from the frat boys and went back to the bar. While Kaitlin waited for their drinks, Abigail crossed off to the back.

"There!" Walton pointed. "Where is she going?"

"Oh, the bathrooms are back there. There's not a camera back there. It's just a hallway. And I legally can't have a camera in the bathroom. I've tried." Ryan caught himself. "Only because kids have stolen the toilets! College kids will freaking steal anything!" Ryan opened his desk drawer, found a couple pistachios and threw them in his mouth. He ate them whole and spat the shells into the trash, again missing badly.

We watched, waiting for Abigail to come back from the bathroom. We kept watching. She didn't come back from the bathroom. We fast-forwarded all the way to the end of the night when the lights came on. She never came back out.

I looked to Walton. "That's when they took her."

"Took who?"

We ignored Ryan and ran to the hallway. We checked both bathrooms. They were disgusting, filled with graffiti, and had no windows. A dead end. We went back to the hallway. We followed it to the end to a door marked FIRE EXIT. ALARM WILL SOUND.

"If she went out there," I suggested, "the alarm would have gone off."

"Actually, that's just a sign," Ryan corrected. "I just put it there so people wouldn't use this door. Most people listen to what signs say. Most people are idiots." Ryan laughed an annoyingly nasal laugh. It sounded like a Western Union telegraph machine. Walton opened the door to a back alley. It was dark, narrow, and empty, save a couple of dumpsters. We couldn't see anyone and nobody could see us. It was the perfect spot for a kidnapping.

It looked like our luck had run out. I didn't see any security cameras back here but I asked Ryan, just in case.

"Actually, there is one. Can't see it, can you? Take a look at that floodlight, looks like a normal floodlight, doesn't it? Uh-uh. Camera. Installed it myself. Someone was stealing kegs of beer from my deliveries and I wanted to see who it was. Haven't caught them yet. But I will."

"You have a camera back here and didn't tell us?" Walton demanded. "You holding out on us, Ryan?"

"What? No! I don't know what's happening. What's happening? Who are you guys?"

Again we ignored Ryan, grabbed him, and led him back to the office. Because he installed the floodlight camera himself, this footage was on his laptop. We scrolled to the end of the night and there was Abigail being loaded into the back of a white van by two men in dark clothing. They wore nondescript hats low on their brows and bandannas covering their mouths and noses. She struggled. Kicked. But it didn't matter. The doors closed and the van peeled off.

"Holy shit," Ryan said. "That girl, she got grabbed. They… They took her. They just fucking took her!" Ryan was panicking. He was clearly not used to high pressure situations.

"Play it again," Walton said calmly.

We watched Abigail being loaded into the back of the white van a second time. And a third. And a fourth. We strained to see the license plate number of the van but we couldn't. Having just been blinded by tear gas certainly didn't help.

"Okay, Ryan," Walton said. "I need all this footage from last night. Both this and the cameras in the bar."

"Wait, I'm not gonna get into trouble for this, am I?"

"Not if you're smart."

"Sure, take this thumb drive," he said. He found a thumb drive in the pistachio drawer and stuck it into the computer USB port and dragged the files into the drive. "Whatever you guys want." He plucked out the drive and handed it to Walton, who promptly gave it to me.

"But we gotta call the cops, right?"

"Wrong," Walton said, putting his hand on his shoulders. "No cops. The only thing you have to do, Ryan, is hire new bouncers. We'll take care of everything else."

"Okay."

"We're gonna come back here tomorrow, if Cal is still working the door that means you didn't listen. If you didn't listen, we got a problem."

"No problem here, man. They're gone."

"Ryan, a great man once said, 'Learn every day like you'll live forever, live every day like you'll die tomorrow.'" Walton stood over him like a beardless Gandalf in a tie-dye T-shirt. "So allow me to modify this quote for this situation. Learn today or die tomorrow."

Chapter 8

We drove back to the hotel in silence. That was unusual. Bill and I talk for a living and our verbosity tended to carry over into our personal lives. But it was late and we were tired. It had been one hell of a night.

Walton was reclining his seat until it was a few degrees off from horizontal. It wasn't far enough but it was as far as it would go. I had almost forgotten about his fight with the bouncers, but clearly Walton had not. His body had seen more action in the last hour than in the previous few decades combined. Bill must have been in quite a bit of pain. But he didn't complain. He never did.

"You okay?" I said, breaking the silence.

"I'm fine." Walton winced and rubbed at his elbow, picking at something. After a confused moment, he held up a tooth. I guess it got embedded in his thick, elephantine skin when he elbowed the second bouncer in the mouth. I watched, horrified, as Walton shrugged and threw the incisor out the window.

"Bill, should I take you to the hospital?"

"Dave, I just need two things. An ice bath and a cold beer. Take me to the hotel."

I drove on. In silence. There was something bothering me. I thought about the incredible fight I had witnessed. *Witnessed.* Maybe that was the problem.

"Bill, just so you know. Outside the bar, I wanted to help, to fight. You know, to have your back, but I was a little blinded from the pepper spray."

"I know."

"But I really wanted to help."

"Sure."

"I mean, it was you against two guys and I just stood there. You needed my help and I just stood there. I should have jumped in. I should have fought. When that happened, how did you decide when to fight? When do you know when to start?"

Walton shook his head.

"Dave, fighting isn't a decision. It's a reaction. When the moment calls for it, you'll know."

I said nothing. I didn't get it. But I had always been a bit of a nerd in an athlete's world. Players and coaches always treated me differently than they treat Bill. I hated it. But I accepted it. I wasn't a full member of their club and never would be.

Walton continued, "Dave, when I'm put in a position like we were tonight, I just remember three things: Preparation. Improvisation. Intimidation." Bill closed his eyes, breathing through his pain. I let him rest.

Preparation. Improvisation. Intimidation.

I had heard those words before. Many times. They were kind of Bill's code during his playing days. A code that originated from three men. All dead. Three men who made up Walton's "Holy

Trinity." Most of the code can be traced back to his lineage as a disciple of perhaps the greatest coach of any sport who ever lived at any time. The numbers certainly support that. No other team showed as much dominance as the 1970s UCLA Bruins of Kareem Abdul-Jabbar and later, Bill Walton.

Coach John Wooden was the embodiment of Midwest Hoosier American uprightness. He was a stickler. But also a revolutionary. He invented drills that are still used by basketball coaches today. For Coach Wooden, the game of basketball was won or lost well before the opening tip. Preparation was far more important than any in- game tactics. Wooden's practices were legendarily tough. So tough that the actual games felt like vacation. That was the point. According to Wooden, failure to prepare was preparing to fail. Wooden was Bill Walton's Obi-Wan.

But he had other influences. Because one day in high school Bill was introduced to the Grateful Dead. And Walton met the other side of his ethos, the circle to the square of John Wooden. His second guru, Jerry Garcia.

Jerry taught Bill the power of improvisation. If the Grateful Dead simply played their album from start to finish, their concerts would be thirty-five minutes long. But they didn't just play the album. They improvised. A lot. That's how a three-minute song became a three-hour exploration of the universe. And that's how Bill lived his life. Anything from taking a spontaneous vacation, to ordering the grilled cheese instead of your usual Cobb salad, to stepping all over your broadcasting partner during a college basketball game to rant about the Missoula Floods. For Bill, the moment of inspiration when a plan was abandoned for the magic of improvisation was called "Following the Dancing Bears" or simply "Jerry." Which I pressed him on one day and he said some new age woo-woo about cosmic consciousness that flowed through all things.

"So like the Force?"

"Yes and no."

"That's not an answer, Bill."

"Yes, it is."

I keep asking about it and he got frustrated.

"Dancing bears, Dave. Either you see them or you don't," he said.

"So are they literal dancing bears? Is this a metaphor or a hallucination?"

"Merely asking that question is proving that you don't get it."

I let it go. By the way, that conversation was during the second half of a nail-biter between BYU and Gonzaga. So, there was that. The hippie aspect. This part, as I've said, lost me. But clearly Jerry was his Yoda.

His third mentor was his best friend. His Han Solo. Maurice Lucas. The most intimidating player in the NBA in the era where fouls were truly not called unless blood hit the floor. Big Luke was a tough kid from the toughest part of a tough town, Pittsburgh, Pennsylvania. His nickname was "The Enforcer" and it was well-earned. A true original. Maurice was the man whose fight with Darryl Dawkins in game two of the 1977 Championship Series swung the momentum away from the heavily favored Philadelphia 76ers to the young, upstart Portland Trail Blazers. And during introductions of the following game, Lucas ran up to Dawkins and shook his hand, psyching out Dawkins and the entire 76ers bench. It was the ultimate psychological checkmate. Intimidation. Lucas and finals MVP Bill Walton won the championship that year. The youngest team ever to do so. Lucas was the oldest player on that team. Walton, one of the youngest. Lucas took Walton under his wing. Taught Walton toughness. What it meant to not back down. What it meant to be a man and a professional. To be tough inside and out. Lessons so valuable for Walton he named one of his sons Luke.

Preparation. Improvisation. Intimidation.

Wooden. Garcia. Lucas.

And Walton being Walton, he really believed that all three men, though quite dead on this earthly plane of existence, were still around. He spoke to them. He felt their presence. He caught glimpses of them in the fringes of life where he said the magic lived. Stars. Moons. Dancing Bears. Again, I never really understood that part.

All three of his mentors were seen in action in Walton's fight with the bouncers. He prepared himself by building an immunity to pepper spray. He improvised, following the Dancing Bears when the second bouncer snuck up on him. And he intimidated Cal into running away without having to throw a single punch. I guess it made sense, but I didn't know how any of it would have helped me. I wasn't prepared. I don't like improvising. And I couldn't intimidate a tuna fish sandwich.

I parked the car in the garage of our very well-appointed hotel. The Hyatt House was a nice place near Key Arena and in the shadow of the Space Needle, Seattle's most famous landmark, built for the

World's Fair in 1962. I had planned to have dinner in its rotating restaurant tonight, but my evening's plans had changed quite drastically since then.

It was 1:30 in the morning. I was exhausted, but to just go to sleep felt weird. Abigail was out there. Somewhere. With guns pointed at her head. We had to keep going.

"Should we take this footage to the video truck and see if we can make out the license plate?"

"Dave, tomorrow… Tomorrow."

"But we have to do something."

"Dave, we can't just keep going all night and all day. We'd burn out. We're Abigail's last best hope. If we want to help her, the smartest thing we can do right now is clear our minds and get some rest.

As Walton unfolded himself out of the car, groaning as his knees cracked, I was reminded of how much pain the big man was in.

"Okay," I reluctantly agreed. "We'll start again first thing tomorrow."

Chapter 9

I showered and put the room service tray holding the remains of my dinner in the hallway, not that there was much left over. The plate was scraped clean. I had savored every bite of the delicious bourbon-glazed salmon, along with the wild rice and salad that came with it. I didn't realize how tired I was until I got in bed. I called my wife to say good night. It was a rule of ours, no matter where I was, I always called to say good night.

And that's what I was doing when Walton walked into my room wearing a hotel robe that barely reached his upper thigh. He resembled an extraordinarily tall Roman centurion on shore leave. He would have looked funny if I wasn't also seeing the scars that went up and down his legs from his multiple surgeries. Knees. Ankles. Feet. There were only a few spots below his waist that weren't made of scar tissue. A few. It looked like he had been attacked by a shark. The sacrifice of a professional athlete.

"Uhh, Bill? What's going on? What are you doing in my room?"

"Dave, I need to borrow your tub." A half dozen hotel employees followed Walton into the room, their arms loaded down with bags of ice. I watched them in amazement.

"Right this way, gentlemen." Walton pointed them into my bathroom and limped slowly behind, carrying the Bluetooth speaker he brought everywhere. I heard the tub start to fill up with cubes as Walton turned the water on.

"Is Bill using your bathroom?" my wife asked, still on the phone.

"Yes."

"Why?

"Good question. Bill! My wife wants to know why you're using my bathroom."

"I'm making kombucha in mine. You won't believe the flavor kits I picked up here. Boysenberry! Oh my goodness. The SCOBY's are pumping, Dave! I'll be good as new in no time."

She laughed. "I don't know how you do it."

"Neither do I," I said.

My wife and I said good night, exchanging those important three words, and I hung up the phone.

"Dave, can I have a beer?" He took two from the mini fridge. I held out my hand just as I realized neither was for me. He went into the bathroom as the hotel employees silently filed out of the room. I heard him ease into the frigid tub, groaning. I tried not to imagine Walton naked in my bathtub, looking like a giant cat in a birdbath.

"Dave," I heard him say through the wall, "what's up with that basketball player?"

"Gonna need you to be more specific than that, Bill."

"The one from New Zealand. The big one. The one who's not throwing it down."

"Ron Barth?"

"Yeah. What's his deal? I need to get some info on him. This is good beer," Walton said of the Heineken he was nursing. "Look Barth up on the Internet, but don't use Google. They track your data. Use DuckDuckGo."

"Bill, I already know everything there is to know about Ron Barth. And do you know why? Because I do my research, Bill. I'm a professional broadcaster and I do my research."

"Okay, Professor Research. Ron Barth, go."

I sighed. Why doesn't he ever ask me this stuff during games?

"Ron Barth, seven feet tall, 240 pounds. Nineteen years old, from Christchurch, New Zealand. Lost family home in an earthquake in 2010. Moved to Auckland. Tough neighborhood. Comes from a large Maori family. Large in both number and size. They're all huge and there's nine of them. Went to Kenny McFadden's basketball academy down there. Prep school at Scots College. As a hobby, he paints."

"Painting houses? Good for him! Jimmy Carter and I once built a house together for Habitat for Humanity. Just two of us in Georgia for a week. It was glorious."

"No, like… painting painting. Like Bob Ross. Rivers and trees and mountains. That kinda painting."

"Interesting. Can you DuckDuckGo some images of his work?"

"Fine, but I'm just using Google."

"They track your data."

"I don't care," I said. "Google is more than welcome to my data."

I found a website of Barth's paintings. It wasn't bad. Not for me, but I'm more of a photograph guy. I love Ansel Adams.

"He's pretty good."

"Describe it to me."

"How?!"

"You're a play-by-play man, Dave. Just call it as you see it!"

"Abstract. Lots of colors. Spirals and faces. Something that looks like ferns. A bird? Kind of a weird bird. It's weird but it's well done. He's pretty talented."

"Thanks, Dave." Then after a pause, "He has the tools to be a great player. He just needs to realize how good he can be. Hey, what do you think of our new producer?"

"She's great."

"You think?" he asked. "I hardly noticed her until today and then it seemed like everything was going wrong."

"Bill, she's great. She's just new and you don't like new things or change."

"Not true. Life is ever-evolving, my friend. I love new things and change."

"You've been listening to the same Grateful Dead songs for forty years."

"New remasters of classic shows are released all the time!"

"Okay, Bill, whatever. Just please try, okay? She's smart. She cares. Give her a chance."

I didn't hear anything but splashing in the tub for a while. Then the music started.

The familiar sounds. The squeaky guitar, the walking-to-nowhere bass, the wah-wah of a stoned keyboard player. I listened. It was better than trying to not listen, which only seemed to make it louder. So, I went to sleep, as I did most nights, to the sound of a rambling guitar solo that seamlessly evolved into an extended jam session that "followed the Dancing Bears" back into a guitar solo. This was Dallas. McFarlin Auditorium. December 26th, 1969. My God, I can even name them now. I hated that I knew that.

Chapter 10

I met Walton in the lobby the next morning. He was holding two paper coffee cups, the kind you find in hotel rooms next to the Keurig machine. I made the mistake of getting my hopes up. I accepted one of the coffees and had a sip. It was cold and wasn't coffee.

"Greetings and blessing, David! How do you like that kombucha? Boysenberry!" Walton said, cheerfully.

"Thanks, Bill. I was hoping for some coffee in my coffee actually." I handed him the cup back. He handed it back to me.

"We have a lot of work to do. You're gonna need these enzymes." I tried another sip. Suppressed a gag.

"What do you think?"

"Um, it tastes... healthy."

"Those are millions and millions of enzymes! Cleaning you from the inside!" I smiled. Pretended to take another sip, suppressed another gag, then surreptitiously dumped the cup into the first garbage can we passed.

Ten minutes later we were in the video truck, which is basically a small mobile television studio. It was 7 A.M. Tipoff was set for 1:00 but people were already there getting ready for the day, which included more games than the two we'd be covering. Bill and I had Washington and USC at 1:00 and a second game at 7:00 between Colorado and Oregon. The video truck was a cramped place. Two rows of computer terminals facing a wall of television screens. Stephanie sat in the middle, busy on her laptop. The vibe had changed drastically from when Bob was in charge. For the better. The farts and cursing had been replaced by a scented candle and the quiet hum of people at work. The crew seemed to be enjoying the transition to Stephanie more than Bill was. She looked up as we came in and took out her AirPods.

"You guys are early. Production meeting is at nine."

"We're not here for the production meeting," Walton said, perhaps too dramatically if he didn't want to arouse attention.

Stephanie shrugged and put her AirPods back in. Walton turned to Nick, the video guy. Nick was young. Early twenties. His dad immigrated from Pakistan in the 80s to attend North Carolina and so, growing up in the Tar Heel state, Nick was a basketball nerd by default. His first words were "Michael Jordan," or so he said. I had my doubts. Nick's dad was an executive with some large corporation in the network's family tree. That may or may not have helped him get the job. Not that I cared. He was good. And trustworthy. When he was not distracted by bidding on sneakers on some shoe auction app.

"Nick, the Video Wizard," Walton boomed. "How are you doing this fine morning, Wizard?"

"Yo, yo, Big Red! What's going on?" Nick said. "Hello, Mr. Pasch."

"Hey, Nick," I said. "How's it going?" I had tried to encourage Nick to give me a nickname too, but after a few nervous attempts ("Pasch Adams," "Pasching Lane," and "Paschtag") we realized it just didn't feel right for either of us. For better or worse, I would always be "Mr. Pasch."

"Check this out, Mr. Pasch. Bidding on these Jordan 1 Retro High OG UNCs." Nick proudly flipped his phone around to show us.

"White and legend blue, baby!"

"They look nice." They did look nice. Not "thousand dollar" nice, but Nick and I had vastly different ideas on how much money a shoe was worth.

"Just remember to put your socks on exactly how I showed you, Video Wizard. No wrinkles. Now, put that away. We need your help."

Walton handed him a thumb drive.

"What's going on?"

"Just a favor for a friend."

Nick inserted the thumb drive and I had him open the file I made earlier that morning, an edited version of the footage that started after Abigail was loaded inside the van. The less Nick knew the better. We only saw the van pull away.

"Right there." Walton pointed at the screen. "We need to know the license plate of that van. We need you to enhance this image. Zoom in."

"Um, No."

"Zoom in. Enhance!"

Nick sighed. Then took his hand away from the mouse. "Look, guys, I can make the score appear at the bottom of the screen. That's kinda the extent of my skill set."

"C'mon, Nick. Just enhance it a little bit," I said.

"Mr. Pasch, that's not a thing. It's like kinda bullshit tech gibberish."

"What do you mean?"

"I mean there is no such technology. There's actually a really funny YouTube video about it, how that trope is used in all these movies and actually it doesn't work because that's not how pixels work. Here, I'll find it, it's hilarious..."

"No. Don't," I said. "We don't have time."

"Well, I'm sorry, guys. I can't do it."

"C'mon, you're the Video Wizard!" Walton pleaded.

"Yeah, you're the only guy who calls me that," Nick said. "All I do is update the score. I have three buttons. One point, two points, three points. My only job is to make sure that the score is right. Like, remember that time in Tucson when I marked a layup as a three-pointer and the score was off for the entire second half and Bob yelled at me in front of everybody? That's all I do. Scores. I'm not the Video Wizard," Nick said, exasperated. "I just never wanted to correct you."

"Maybe I can help." We turned around. Stephanie was right behind us. I didn't realize she was that close and by the pause, neither did Walton.

"Stephanie, eavesdropping is not only rude, it's a breach of privacy. In fact, the Supreme Court has consistently—"

"It's a small room, Bill, and your voice literally bounces off the walls. And since I couldn't possibly help but overhear, you need the license plate of that van, yes?"

"Yes," I said. Walton blinked.

"Okay. Let me give it a go. I can probably do it." Walton was still for a long time. Then he shrugged.

"Okay. Let's see what you can do." Walton signaled for Nick to give her the thumb drive.

"By the way," Stephanie said. "What's this for?"

"It's a personal matter. We just need to know the license plate."

She looked both of us in the eye and took a deep breath.

"All right," she said, with a sigh. "Okay. That's cool."

"And we need to stress that this needs to be done in a sensitive manner," I said.

"I can keep a secret." Stephanie smiled.

"Great."

"Okay. I'll have it for you by the end of the game."

"See you at the meeting. 9:00." She started to walk off, then stopped. Turned around. "You know, it's funny, I really thought you two didn't hang out together outside work. I kinda thought you hated each other."

Stephanie chuckled, grabbed her tan bag, and left the truck.

"Do you think she can actually do it?" I asked.

Nick laughed.

"What's so funny?"

"You guys really don't know the deal with her, do you?"

"No, Nick, I do not know the deal with her. I don't know the deal with her at all," Walton said. Nick smirked.

"Dude, Stephanie is insane. Her LinkedIn reads like a thriller. I bookmarked it! She was a war correspondent producer. Hot zones. Boots on the ground. Embedded. Christiane Amanpour typa shit."

I was shocked. This was the first I was hearing about any of this. "How'd she end up here?"

"She got married. Had a kid. Came back stateside. Wanted to raise her daughter in a more secure environment than, you know, Syria."

"And she chose college basketball?" Walton asked. Nick shrugged. "Absurd!"

"She's a little overqualified for this job, to be honest." I thought out loud.

"Ya think?" Nick scoffed. "We do college basketball. She was out there covering revolutions, coups, drug cartels, wars! How cool is that?"

"I don't think war is cool, Nick," Walton said. "I don't think war is very cool at all. I also don't think it's 'cool' the network saddled us with a producer who has zero basketball experience." Nick kept scrolling down her LinkedIn.

"Oh, Big Red. You really don't know anything about Stephanie, do you?"

"I know she loves interrupting my train of thought with meaningless statistics." Nick clicked on a picture. It was Stephanie, in the 90s, hair pulled back with a green headband across her forehead. Basketball in her hands. "She played point guard for Notre Dame in 2002."

"Really, how come I never heard of her?"

"Bill, you don't know the names of players in the games we call," I reminded him.

"She got a full ride after a standout career at Camden High School in New Jersey, but blew her knee out two months into her freshman season. She spent the rest of her career on the bench as an assistant to the assistant coaches. And, you know, getting a communications degree from freakin' Notre Dame."

"I wonder why she didn't mention this before," Walton said.

"Maybe," I suggested, "because you haven't spoken to her other than to tell her to talk less?"

Walton paused, unsure.

"Maybe. Maybe... I might be wrong about her." Walton seemed reflective. I was slightly surprised. It's not often the big man will admit to being wrong about someone.

"Maybe," he repeated.

"Look at this clip of her hitting a game winner in the preseason NIT." Nick double-clicked his way to a video site. There was young Stephanie taking the ball full court, running and dribbling with blinding speed, then stopping on a dime to pop a jump shot that knocked Indiana out of the tournament. "She's been shot at and she's got a jump shot? What a legend!" Nick grinned. I looked at Walton with an "I told you so" glint in my eye.

"Don't say it," said Walton.

"I didn't say anything."

"You were going to, Pasch. I could tell."

"I didn't say anything."

"Okay," Walton said. "I'll say it. I was wrong about our new producer."

Chapter 11

We had two hours before the production meeting. Stephanie was working on the only lead we had, the license plate of the van that took Abigail. Walton checked in with Phil Engels. He and his wife Helen had heard nothing more from the kidnappers. I couldn't tell if that was good news or bad news. Bill said they sounded shaken and hadn't slept at all last night. I couldn't blame them.

So we had two hours with nothing to do. Well, I couldn't do nothing. Bill took another ice bath, thankfully in his own tub this time. His body was still recovering from last night's action. I sat at the tiny desk in my room, opened my laptop, and took another look at the security footage from the Smokeshow. I watched every frame from every camera in the bar, noticing stuff I hadn't seen before. Most of it useless. I watched the vampire lady steal a small fortune from Ryan. Apparently, if you paid in cash that money was all hers. I saw a chubby boy vomit all over the floor and, a little later, Ryan shuffling over to clean it up with a mop and bucket. Ryan slipped and almost fell down in the vomit. I chuckled along with the kids in the bar. There was Kaitlin coming back from the bar with another round of drinks, looking around for Abigail. But Abigail was already in the back of a van headed God knows where.

I watched Kaitlin circle the bar, looking in every nook and corner for her roommate. There was Cal and the other bouncer running in to break up another fight. Wait a second. *The fight.*

I forgot about the altercation between Abigail and that spiky haired boy. I rewound the footage and switched cameras to find when he entered the bar. He was alone. Clearly looking for Abigail. He spotted her dancing with the frat boys and headed right over. Then the argument. He towered over the two frat boys. Tall. Broad shouldered. Wait a second.

I switched over to the other file that had the footage of Ryan's secret floodlight camera in the back alley. To the two men throwing Abigail into the van. You couldn't see hair under the hats and bandannas, but one of the men was tall and broad shouldered. Just like the spiky haired boy. I paused the two videos and shrank them so I could see them side by side on my screen. I felt a tingle run up and down my spine. It was a match.

I shouted for Walton to come over. Moments later he was out of his bath and back in his centurion robe, dripping water all over my floor. I showed him the two videos and he agreed with me. One of the kidnappers could easily have been the spiky haired boy. We called Abigail's roommate, Kaitlin. She didn't answer. It was a little past 8:30 in the morning, still pretty early for a college kid, so I texted her to call me. Twenty minutes later, Walton and I had her on speakerphone in my hotel room.

"Kaitlin," I asked. "Who was that guy Abigail got into a fight with at the Smokeshow?"

"Oh God. I forgot. Wait, how did you know about that?"

"We saw some security footage of the night she disappeared."

"Oh. Did you see who grabbed her?!"

"Yes and no. We can't see much, just that one of the kidnappers looks a lot like that boy with the spiky hair. Who was that?"

"That would be Kern, her ex. Total tool. Oh man, you think Kern did this? That's crazy, but actually not that crazy because he is the worst. I mean, you saw what happened. He was always doing that kind of shit."

"Kaitlin, Bill Walton here," he said, very unnecessarily. Who else could it possibly have been, shouting an inch away from the speakerphone mic? "Did she mention anything to you? Did anything unusual happen recently between her and this Kern character?"

"Not really. I mean, she broke up with him a couple days ago but that's not unusual. They've broken up a few times and they've only been dating for like a month. But this time she said it was really over and I believed her. He like, yelled at a waitress in front of her because there was cheese on his hamburger. Or there wasn't cheese on his cheeseburger. I forget. Whatever. The point is: Kern's a lunatic."

"Kern? Is that his first name?"

"Hmmm. I actually don't know. Everybody just calls him Kern."

"Do you really think he's capable of something like this?"

"Yeah. He's a fucking asshole. I mean he's an NRA, men's rights, red pill, right-wing douchebag. He grew up hunting. It's fucking disgusting."

"Kaitlin, that night at the Smokeshow," I said, trying to steer the conversation back on track. "What did Abigail and Kern fight about?"

"What else? Kern saw her dancing with another other guy and freaked out. Abigail told him they weren't dating anymore and that she wasn't his fucking property and he went nuts."

I asked if she had Kern's phone number.

"No. Gross," she said, before adding, "I don't even follow him on Instagram. It's all pictures of steak and guns. Disgusting."

We looked Kern up on Instagram and there he was, at a gun range firing an Uzi. This was one intense kid.

Walton, no stranger to "the Gram," as he called it, pointed to the screen.

"That's a live video. Kern's there right now."

Chapter 12

Stephanie ran a tight ship. The production meeting started on time and was done by 9:20. I was grateful. Meetings with Bob tended to run long, often sidetracked by his screaming at an underling or regaling us with tales from the "good old days," which would easily get Walton going as well. Production meetings with Bob had lasted hours; she had us out of there in twenty minutes. Chalk up another point for Stephanie. Walton and I raced over to the shooting range, hoping Kern hadn't run out of bullets.

Tactical Seattle was a gun range in a converted warehouse not far from downtown. I knew from trips like these with my father-in-law we couldn't just waltz into a room full of people shooting guns. There were forms to be filled out, guns to be rented, bullets to be bought. We walked inside and were greeted by a bored, attractive brunette with a difficult-to-place European accent. She flipped through an old copy of *Guns & Ammo* as we filled out our forms. If I had to guess I'd say she was depressed or stoned. This being Seattle, the odds were likely it was both.

We headed to the back and opened a soundproof door that led into a small vestibule. Once that door closed, we were buzzed through a second soundproof door that led into the shooting range. Even with our earmuffs on, the constant barrage of gunshots was overpowering. There were about twenty shooting booths and about half of them were filled. We saw Kern's spiky hair and broad shoulders at the end of the row. He and a few friends took up the last two booths, spraying paper targets with fully automatic machine guns. I didn't know what kind; they were far out of my father-in-law's league. He preferred something closer to what Wyatt Earp would have carried.

Kern was in the last booth trying to control the Uzi he had brandished on Instagram. The gun roared like a tin lion. Kern finished the clip, then flipped the switch for the mechanical pulley to bring back the target, which was a man holding a woman hostage. Bullet holes were punctured all over the paper. Including the hostage's face.

We walked up to Kern. I glanced over at his friends, looking for someone with a body type similar to the second man who grabbed Abigail. None of them seemed quite right. The other man in the security footage was taller and wider than any of these boys.

I looked at Kern as he admired his paper target. Could he have taken Abigail and held her hostage? Punishment for breaking up with him? He and his friends certainly had access to the guns that were pointed at her head in the video.

"Kern? Kern! We need to talk to you!" Walton's booming voice overpowered the earmuffs and the gunfire. Kern turned around. If he recognized Walton, he didn't show it. But there was something about a seven-foot man that grabs people's attention.

"What do you want?!"

"We need to talk to you!" Walton repeated.

"About what?!" The barrel was pointed upward, still smoking. Kern seemed to have proper gun etiquette at least.

"Can we go somewhere quiet so we can talk?!"

"Are you guys cops?!"

"No! We're not cops. We just want to talk. Can we step outside?"

"We can talk here. We're talking right now," Kern screamed. He gently laid the Uzi on its side and hung up a fresh paper target, another drawing of a man holding a gun to a woman's head. A disturbing reminder of the video from the kidnappers. He hit the switch and the target glided down range.

"We were told you used to date Abigail Engels."

He popped another clip in the Uzi.

"Not anymore!" He cocked the bolt and fired the entire magazine at the paper target ten feet away. Shredding it in seconds. Bits of paper fell like cherry blossoms to the concrete floor. Up close I saw Kern's spiky hair was the result of a large amount of hair gel. He wore a polo shirt and frayed plaid shorts that looked expensively frayed. Apple watch with a leather band around his wrist. His friends all wore the same basic rich kid uniform of jeans and boat shoes that matched their polos. They sensed trouble and gathered around Kern, which empowered him. Not that a rich white kid holding an Uzi needed much empowering.

"Son, put the gun down and talk to us!" Walton said.

"Hey, you're not my dad and you're not the cops. This is weird. Get out of here, Penn and Teller. Go do some magic!"

Kern and his friends laughed. Penn and Teller. Not bad. So far, that was Kern's best shot of the day.

"What did you do after they threw you out of the Smokeshow Tuesday night?!" Walton blurted. Kern was surprised. As was I. He didn't expect us to know about that. I didn't expect Walton to reveal that we did. Kern quickly gathered himself.

"Oh, she told you about that, huh? Well, thanks to that bitch, those bouncers cut up my fake ID and handed me over to the fucking cops. I was in the drunk tank until morning. You ever been in the drunk tank? It's not fun. So fuck her and fuck you, man. Get the fuck out of here!"

Kern had been arrested? Among the barrage of profanity, Kern had given us an airtight alibi. If he was in jail that night, which would be easy to verify, he couldn't have been the big, broad-shouldered guy in the video. This was a complete waste of time. Time we didn't have. We got out of there. Kern and his friends ignored our goodbyes and Walton and I walked out to a hail of gunfire behind us.

We returned the bullets and our unfired weapon, a Remington M1911, to the woman behind the counter and left the shooting range. Just before we got to the car, Kern ran out of the building and caught up to us in the parking lot. He checked over his shoulder, making sure none of his friends followed him out.

"Look, um, I should tell you the other night, you know when me and Abi got in a fight? I was hammered. I had already had like a million beers when I saw her Instagram from the Smokeshow and ran over there."

"What Instagram?" Walton said, grabbing his phone. "I follow Abigail and she hasn't posted anything in weeks." He held up the selfie Abigail took while hiking on a rare, blue sky day in Seattle with Mount Rainier in the background. Kern laughed.

"That's the account her family knows about. I follow her Finsta."

"Finsta?" Walton asked, confused.

"Fake-Instagram. You post your real pictures just for your friends to see. It's a private account. Everyone does it." Kern clicked on Abigail's "Finsta" and scanned through pictures of her drinking, partying, and doing all the things parents didn't want to know their children were doing. He landed on a picture Abigail posted the night she was kidnapped. She and Kaitlin smushed together, celebrating their entrance into the bar.

"Huh," Kern said. "She hasn't posted since that night. That's weird. Does she have a new Finsta I don't know about? Shit."

"So that's how you knew she was at the Smokeshow?" I asked.

"Yeah. One second she breaks up with me, the next she's at the Smokeshow dancing with some assholes. I went nuts. But I didn't hurt Abigail, I never would. I love her. I think, maybe." He went on, voice trembling and cracking. He seemed a middle schooler to me then.

"So, do me a favor and tell her I'm sorry. And I've changed. I haven't had a beer since that night."

"Kern," I said, "that was two nights ago. That means you were sober for one night?"

"And day," Kern noted proudly. "Tell Abi she should call me. Could call me. If she wants. You know, when you talk to her or whatever."

"Okay, Kern. We'll let her know," I said.

"Did Abigail happen to say anything to you lately?" Walton added. "Anything unusual? Anything that made her nervous?"

Kern's face fell. It finally dawned on him that we weren't there because of the fight at the Smokeshow.

"What's going on? Is she okay? Is she in trouble?"

"No, no. She's fine. We're just looking into something," I said, vaguely. I didn't want to tip our hand about what happened. Finding her would not be any easier if we had to deal with a well-armed, white knight boyfriend and his Abercrombie army.

"Well, she never told me anything like that," Kern said, thinking. "If something was going on, she would have definitely told her best friend."

"Kaitlin?"

"No, not her roommate, her best friend. Sara Soho."

He gave us Sara's number, we bid Kern goodbye and got in the Chrysler 300. I started the car and rolled down my window. Kern watched us with his puppy dog eyes. He still had his shooting earmuffs around his neck.

"Hey, is Kern your first name or last name?"

"Second middle," said Kern. Then he turned and walked back inside.

As we drove away Walton said, "Didn't see that coming."

Chapter 13

We met Sara Soho in the parking lot of a Dairy Queen a few miles from campus. She was wearing cowboy boots, tight jeans, and a puffy coat while sitting on the bed of a brand-new pickup truck that was clearly never used to haul anything. It was 10:30 in the morning and she was eating a Blizzard and smoking a cigarette. Not exactly the breakfast of champions.

"Where the fuck is Abigail?" Sara asked. Her phone had some kind of case on it that made it look like a rabbit. "She's not returning my texts, she's not watching my Insta stories, is she mad at me?"

"How long have you two known each other?"

"Since forever. We've been friends since like fourth grade." Sara finished the Blizzard and popped a stick of gum in her mouth. She was still smoking. "Seriously, where is she? Did she have a breakdown or something?"

"No, no. Abigail's fine. We just need to know if she said anything to you recently. Anything unusual. Someone making her nervous, or following her or something like that."

Her eyes went wide.

"Oh my God. Did she get kidnapped or something? Did she get taken?!" She looked at us. She must have seen something in our faces.

"She did! She got kidnapped, didn't she?!"

"No, no, she's fine," I lied, I thought convincingly.

"Bullshit," she pressed. "Abi is my best friend. What's going on? Tell me the truth right now or I'm calling the cops."

Walton and I checked in with each other and nodded.

"Sarah, Abigail's father got a video from people who took her, demanding a very large ransom," I said. "We're trying to figure out who did it but Sara, and this is very important, we can't go to the cops." Sara looked at us. Then burst into laughter.

"Oh my God." She clapped. "That bitch kidnapped her damn self. Bet!"

I told Sara I didn't think that was true, but she laughed even louder.

"Last week she asked her dad if she could come with me and my family to Berlin for Christmas and he said no. You shoulda seen her. She was furious."

Walton and I looked at each other as Sara went on.

"Trust me, she's fucking with her dad to get back at him."

"Do you really think Abigail would kidnap herself?"

"Absolutely. She was always complaining about money. Her parents kept her on a tight budget. Her dad wouldn't even give her a credit card for emergencies and he's loaded. He's like some big shot. Trust me. She faked that shit. What's the ransom? A thousand dollars and a Tiffany bracelet? Suck my ass. When you see her, tell her to call me. I'm outta here. It's too early for this shit."

Sara hopped off the truck and was about to leave when Walton nudged me.

"Dave, show her the video."

I pulled out my phone. Phil had shared the video with me. I'd watched it a dozen times, hoping to pull some kind of clue from it. I didn't. The video didn't change, yet it got worse every time. I played it for Sara, who leaned in, ready to enjoy a show. The moment Sara saw Abigail scream, the color drained from her cheeks. By the end of the video, she was crying.

"Turn it off. Jesus Christ. That's definitely not fake. I've known Abigail for a long time. And I know how she lies. To her dad, her teachers, her boyfriends. To me. She's pretty good at it, too. But not that fucking good. That's not fake. She's really scared." Sara started to cry as if she realized what that meant.

"Oh God. Who the fuck did that to her?!"

"We don't know," Walton assured her. "But I promise you we're going to find out and get her back."

"Is there anything else you can tell us, Sara?" I prompted. "Anything at all you can think of?"

"No. I mean, one thing... That video was shot on a boat."

"How do you know that?" Walton asked. She grabbed my phone, turned down the sound so she wouldn't have to hear her friend scream again, and replayed the video. We watched for a few seconds.

"There," Sara said. "Do you see?" Indeed the frame rocked back and forth very slightly.

"I saw that," I said. "I thought it was just the person holding the camera."

"No. That's how a boat would rock. I'm from Seattle, dude. I grew up on boats."

Moments later Sara drove off in her truck. We waved and walked back to the car. We had a game to call.

"A boat. Well, that's something," Walton said.

"It's not much."

"Better than nothing."

"Bill, all we know is that after she was kidnapped she was put on a boat. Which means we narrowed down her current location to anywhere between Lake Washington and Japan."

Chapter 14

"The Washington Huskies are rolling and there is nothing USC can do about it! Another three-pointer for Hitchcock!" The crowd was roaring, the student section jumping.

"Dave! Dante Hitchcock is on fire! He's torching the entire court! The creativity, the improvisation, he's like Jimi Hendrix lighting his guitar aflame. Foxy Lady!"

"Hitchcock is five for six from downtown this half."

"He's tossing in three-pointers like they were freshly caught Alaskan salmon at the Seattle fish market. Pike Place market! What a place. The original Starbucks! Tiny doughnuts!"

"USC needs to find a way to stop Hitchcock before their season goes down the drain."

"Well, they certainly don't need to worry about stopping Ron Barth. Barth is stopping himself! He's having another awful game. Abysmal!"

"Ah, I don't know if I would say Barth has had an awful game."

"It's a tragedy, Dave. Hitchcock has pulled the defense out to the perimeter. The lane is wide open and Barth is still putting up weak fadeaway jumpers and soft marshmallow hook shots. It makes me sad for humanity. I weep for Ron Barth and I weep for us all."

"Gee, Bill. You might want to go easy on the kid." I try not to criticize amateur athletes. They were just kids after all. Bill had a different philosophy.

"Whenever I see a big man not throwing it down, I feel like we all are not throwing it down. It's a reflection of humanity's failures! Hiroshima! I want to see him moving like the Missoula Floods, the unstoppable power of the elements! Instead we see a young man befuddled by his own talent, two roads divided in a yellow wood and he is taking the road not dunked on! A tragedy on an unfathomable scale is unfolding before our very eyes."

"He does have twelve rebounds, Bill."

"I haven't seen it."

"Okay guys," Stephanie's voice came into our headsets. "We're putting up the Cascadia Community Bank Numbers of the Game. And… go." The graphic came on the screen.

"Well, Bill, it just so happens that the Cascadia Community Bank Numbers of the Game are all about the Husky big man. As we see here, Barth's scoring is way down compared to the regular season although he rebounded pretty well today."

"Why are you showing the audience the number of rebounds he has?" Walton screamed. "Why not show them the number of rebounds he doesn't have?! Get those numbers off the screen, Stephanie! Stop stuffing numbers down our throats. Numbers don't matter!"

"That was our Cascadia Community Bank Stat of the Game. Cascadia Community Bank: Numbers matter."

"No, they don't."

"Bill, stop saying numbers don't matter! That is literally the opposite of our sponsor's motto!" Stephanie sounded increasingly distressed in our headphones.

"You know what matters? Letters. Letters matter. Two in particular: W and L!"

On the court, Hitchcock drained another three-pointer and USC thankfully called a timeout that took us to a commercial. We all needed a break.

The commercial break didn't help. The last five minutes of the game was a poor display of basketball and broadcasting. Bill went on an endless rant about the lack of bike infrastructure in the United States and Stephanie responded by peppering the screen with more and more stats and billboards than was probably necessary. At one point I think she made up a sponsor, because I had never seen the Flabersham Carpets Wall-to-Wall Defensive Play of the Game before.

It certainly wasn't our finest moment on the air, while on the court the bench players for both teams took turns missing open jump shots in garbage time. Of course, "garbage time" is a term I would never use on air. But it's a fact, the final ten minutes of a blowout is a professional broadcaster's nightmare.

"USC misses another long three, that was, uh…" Who was that? I was blanking on the name of the benchwarmer USC had just put in the game. Stephanie rescued me, quickly putting the name in my ear. At least someone was paying attention to the game.

"That was Dan Sher. A junior from Jacksonville who averages… no points a game. He hasn't scored a single point this season? Wow. Bill? Any comment?"

"No."

This was officially a disaster.

"Okay, we have some more numbers, Bill," I segued. "I know how much you like those…"

"What do numbers tell about heart? You can't measure the heart of a human being." Bill crossed his arms.

"Well, you can measure the beats per minute," I pointed out.

"So what? What does that tell you?"

"It literally measures the strength of the human heart."

"No, it doesn't," Walton said. "The most factual book in America is the census! But what does it tell you about the truth of America? Nothing! Less than nothing! Men lie. Women lie. Numbers lie. The ball doesn't. You know who said that? Rasheed Wallace, a great basketball mind. And a good friend."

"This will likely be the third time in five years that USC has been knocked out at this stage of the tournament. Stephanie, our producer, has provided us with some pretty informative stats, Bill. Care to comment on those?"

"Dave, please, let's get back to the game."

"Bill, I do believe that is the first time you've ever said that to me."

The crowd cleared out pretty quickly after the game. Following a blowout, nobody lingers. Walton signed a few autographs. Normally he'd spend hours happily signing every autograph that was asked of him, which was just fantastic when we had dinner reservations. Walton would sign anything. Literally anything. If you handed Bill Walton a CVS receipt and a crayon, he'd sign it. Fortunately, there were only a few autograph seekers tonight.

Nobody ever asked for my autograph except for the real college basketball broadcasting nerds. And there were very, very few of them. We hurried back to the dressing room. Walton slowed down just long enough to insult the referees for the afternoon's game.

"Gentlemen, that was a horribly officiated game."

"Fuck you, Walton," they said, in unison, while flipping him the bird.

Walton walked away, satisfied. We got into our dressing room. I washed my face in the sink as Walton checked his phone. Phil texted a few times. No new information. There was a knock at the door and Stephanie didn't wait for an answer. She just walked in. Walton greeted her as he was zipping up his fleece pullover.

"Stephanie, good to see—"

"Shut up, Bill." We stood there, shocked.

"First off. If you call me out during a broadcast one more time, I'm gonna break your other foot. If you want to criticize me? No problem. Tell me I'm doing a bad job? I can take it. But you do that after the game. Calling me out on air is just bad broadcasting. So cut the garbage."

I smiled. I wish someone was filming this. She turned to me.

"And Pasch, I need better from you too!"

"What did I do?!"

"I don't want to hear it, Dave! I just want you do to better."

"Thank you," Walton said. "We can all agree on that."

I bit my tongue. Best to just let things go. Besides, I suspected Stephanie was making sure not to just scold Walton and leave me as the golden child. I had to respect her for not driving a wedge between two broadcasters. Stephanie assessed us and nodded, satisfied.

"Secondly, I got your dang license plate." She took a manila folder out of her backpack. "I sent the footage to a government contact I have. They couldn't magically enhance the image, because that's nonsense. But they were able to access the traffic cameras in the surrounding area. And about a minute after it left the alley, your white van ran a red light a few blocks from the bar."

She opened the folder to show us screenshots she had printed up. "See? It's the same van, you can tell by dented bumper."

She then showed us a crystal clear shot of the van's license plate, taken from a traffic camera as it ran the red light.

"Wow. Great!" Walton cheered. He seemed to have completely forgotten the tongue lashing he had just received. "This is perfect, Stephanie. Thank you. I'll just text the plate number to my great friend Sergeant Galloway of the San Francisco PD. Don't worry, he's not like regular cops. He's a cool—"

"No need, Bill," Stephanie interrupted. "I already traced the plate." Walton looked crestfallen as she handed me another piece of paper from the folder.

"The van is owned by a mister Guy Gibby who lives south of town, near Tacoma. His address is right there."

My heart leapt. We had them. Walton was clearly as invigorated as I was.

"Let's do this, Pasch. Thank you, Stephanie!" Walton said, as he headed out the door.

"Guys, wait. There's something else!" Walton was already in the hallway. I shot Stephanie an apologetic look and followed him out.

"Hey! Where are you two going?! Walton!? Pasch!?" Her voice echoed down the hall. The last words I heard as we left the building were, "You better be back for the 7:00 game!" Once outside, I had to jog to catch up to Walton. Even on two bad legs, the big man could cover a lot of ground in a hurry.

Chapter 15

The skies were undulating ripples of grey and the drizzle was light but steady. I turned on the seat warmers and kicked up the heat. The windshield wipers were automatic as they sensed the precipitation on the windshield.

"Seattle," I grumbled as I looked at the endless grey clouds above us. "They should always have the Pac-12 Tournament someplace warm. They should have it in Vegas every year."

"C'mon, Dave, the location of the tournament rotates. As it should. You can't host a collegiate tournament in Sin City! These are student athletes, not bachelor party degenerates! Besides, the rain is good for you. It's great for the skin. Vitamin R! Liquid sunshine!"

"No, it's not. It's depressing. Every other billboard is for suicide prevention or drug addiction. Obviously, this place is depressing."

"It's only depressing if you're depressed. Dave! Feel the rain! Breathe it in!" Bill pushed a button and slid back the sunroof, stretching his arms out to their maximum reach overhead. He lifted his face and opened his mouth and stuck his tongue out like a dog lapping up the raindrops.

"Please don't get the interior of this rental wet, Bill. I don't want to incur the extra cleaning fee," I said, pushing the button to close the roof. Walton pulled his arms inside just in time.

We followed the navigation to a trailer park on the outskirts of Tacoma. Most of the RVs looked like they had been there for a long time. We parked near a run-down double-wide at the back of the park, near a chain-link fence. A Yamaha motorcycle that seemed like it was in working order was splayed next to half a Harley that definitely wasn't. The "lawn" in front of the trailer had way more scattered parts and tools than grass.

Walton banged on the side of the trailer with a ham-sized fist until a voice inside finally yelled, "I'm coming, motherfucker!"

The door opened but the screen door stayed closed. Behind it stood a man who looked like he'd woken up from a two-day nap after a three-day bender. He was around forty years old. Rail thin with shaggy red hair, a blank expression, and an unfortunate overbite.

"Guy Gibby?"

"Yeah. And if you're from the bank, fuck off. I already said I ain't interested in no refinance bullshit."

"We're not from the bank," I said.

"Holy shit, you're Bill Walton!" Gibby said. Walton nodded modestly.

"What are you doing here? Did I win a contest or something?"

"No, you didn't win a contest. Look, Guy."

"Call me Gibby."

"Fine. Gibby. We have some questions about your van."

"My van? That shit got stolen a week ago, it's gone. Yeah man, you can't trust anyone around here. Crackheads, smokers, and junkers. If it ain't nailed down, boy, I tell ya. You can kiss it goodbye."

I sighed. This was disappointing. Two minutes ago we thought we had the guy who did it. And now we were back to square one. We had to find out more. Maybe Gibby saw who took the van? Great. Now we were investigating a kidnapping and a stolen vehicle.

"Do you mind if we come in and ask you a few more questions?" Walton said.

"Nah, Bill Fucking Walton, come on in. You were my favorite player when I was a kid. Because we both had red hair. I was too young for you on the Trail Blazers, but the Celtics? That was my fucking team! Holy shit. Bill Walton! Get in here!"

He pushed open the screen door to let us in.

"Sorry, it's kinda messy."

This was an understatement. Gibby's trailer was a disaster. The carpet was a dull, yellow shade. Maybe it started as white many, many years ago. Full ashtrays were scattered about like dirty little hedgehogs. It seemed everywhere was the smoking section. The entire trailer smelled like hot dog water. I did not enjoy being there.

"Maid's week off?" I asked.

"I don't have a maid," Gibby said.

No one ever gets my jokes.

"So what's this all about? Hey, do you know where my van is or something?" Gibby asked.

"No. Sorry, Gibby. We don't," Walton said. "Do you have any idea who took it?"

"No, man. No idea. There one night, gone the next morning. Just another shitty thing to happen to me in a series of shitty things that makes up my shitty fucking life," Gibby said in a moment of self-pity. Or clarity. It quickly passed with a belch.

Gibby seemed convincing, but his nervous lack of eye contact told me he was holding something back. He went to the kitchen and grabbed a bottle of domestic from the fridge. He twisted the cap and took a long draw.

There was a old laptop open on the couch. I pivoted my way over to see what was on it. A pornographic video was frozen on his computer screen. A blurry frame of skin. So this is what he was doing when we knocked. Did I shake his hand when I came in? Oh no. Now I need to wash my hands but I feared even the soap in this trailer would cause more harm than good. Gibby wandered back from the kitchen with an already half drunk beer and lit a smoke, which certainly wasn't going to improve the air quality in the room. I wanted to finish this as quickly as possible.

"Gibby, just a few more questions about the van. If you were here when it was stolen… Didn't you hear it start up? A van like that probably makes a lot of noise."

"Yeah, nah, I didn't hear it. Heavy sleeper. And, you know what, I forgot. I actually got some shit to do." Gibby grabbed a bag of garbage and threw it next to some more garbage near the kitchen.

"Y'all should probably get goin'."

I looked to Walton, who was over by the stereo hi-fi system thumbing through Gibby's crates of albums. He held up Pink Floyd's *Wish You Were Here*.

"Pink Floyd. Not for me," Walton said. "Too theatrical."

"Yeah, that's not even mine. A buddy of mine left that here."

Walton thumbed through a few more albums before lifting up one by REO Speedwagon. Walton cocked an eyebrow.

"You dig the Wagon?" he asked.

"Hell yeah, I dig the fucking Wagon," Gibby said. Cigarette dangling from his lips.

"Same, friend. 'Roll With the Changes.' A personal favorite..." he said. Then Walton closed his eyes and began to recite the lyrics, slowly like he was reading from an ancient scroll of poetry.

"As soon as you are able, woman I am willing. To make the break that we are on the brink of. My cup is on the table, my love is spilling. Waiting here for you to take and drink of. So if you are tired of the same old story. Oh, turn some pages. I will be here when you are ready."

"To roll with the changes." Gibby nodded.

"Roll with the changes," Walton said, reverently. I didn't know Walton was a big REO Speedwagon fan. But the breadth and depth of his musical knowledge always impressed me.

"Did you ever get a chance to see them live?" Walton asked.

Gibby closed his eyes and took a sharp drag. "Yeah, my dad took me to go see them at the Tacoma Dome when I was a kid."

"He sounds like a good dad," Walton said.

"He was a real piece of shit," Gibby said. He exhaled a cloud of smoke into the middle of the room. "But that Speedwagon show... that was a great night. He bought me a hot dog and soda. Then he tried to sneak a bottle from one of the bars and security guards chased us. We ran to our car before they could get us. It's my fondest memory of him."

Walton said nothing. Gibby looked out the window to the road out back.

"Look, Gibby. Whoever took your van kidnapped the daughter of a very good friend of Bill's. They're holding her for a ten million dollar ransom."

"Holy shit!"

"We'd really appreciate anything you can tell us about the van or who might have taken it."

Bill stepped forward. He had to hunch over in the trailer. He put his hands on Gibby's narrow shoulders.

"Please, Gibby. She's my goddaughter. We just want to get her back home safely. No one has to get in trouble. Whoever took her can keep the money. We just want the girl."

Gibby was clearly conflicted. He thought. Hard. Always painful to see someone so visibly thinking. Walton sensed Gibby was on the precipice of opening up to us. What he said next pushed him right over the edge.

"Gibby, I'm going to tell you the same thing Larry Bird said to me right before Game Six of the '86 Finals: Come on, Big Red. I need ya."

The words melted Gibby's ginger heart. The mention of Larry Bird, by Bill Walton, in his trailer, destroyed any hesitation Gibby had to tell us everything he knew about that van.

"Okay, I definitely shouldn't tell you guys this, but here's the deal. The van wasn't stolen. I'm a prospect in an MC, you know, a motorcycle club. I'm kinda, you know, like, the first level or whatever. Just payin' my dues 'til I get my patch. And one day the head dude, Ike, he walked up to me and says he needs my van. I handed him the keys and didn't ask any questions. If you knew Ike, you'd understand."

I couldn't believe it. What I thought was a dead end had just turned into a five-lane highway leading right to Abigail.

"So Ike had the van last Tuesday night?" I blurted.

"Yeah, I guess. I wasn't there. That's way above my pay grade."

Walton suddenly looked very determined.

"Gibby, where can we find this Ike?"

"Find Ike? Shit, why would you want to find Ike? Stay away from him. Trust me. He's a bad dude, man. I mean, he's super cool. But you don't want to fuck with Ike. You don't want to talk to Ike. You don't want to look Ike in the eye. Just steer clear of that dude."

"Gibby, I was at Altamont. Trust me, I'm not afraid of any biker."

"Oh, he's way more than a biker. Hates that term, actually. Ike's a big deal around here, man. He's got his hands in all the cookie jars. If you snort, shoot, smoke, or fuck in King Country, he's getting a taste. And nobody, I mean nobody, fucks with Ike."

"Gibby, don't worry about us, we'll be fine. Just tell us where to find this Ike," Walton insisted. I was starting to have doubts this was a good idea. Gibby shrugged.

"He owns a bar called the Levee, he's there all the time. I'm sure he's there right now." Panic gripped Gibby's eyes. "But, hey man, don't tell him I told you anything. In fact, don't mention me at all." He cleared his throat. "Please?"

Walton nodded. "Of course, Gibby. Just one more thing. What does Ike look like?"

Gibby gave a dark chuckle. "Just look for the big motherfucker with two grenades on his belt."

"Grenades? C'mon, Gibby," said Walton.

"If I'm lying, I'm dying," Gibby said. "Two live grenades. And let me tell you something, brother. There used to be three."

Chapter 16

We headed south following the navigational directions to Renton, a town close to the Sea-Tac airport. We got to an industrial area near the freeway where the streets looked like they haven't been cleaned for a while. Broken bottles sparkled like diamonds in the gutter. The clouds parted for a few hours but the trees sagged from the rain.

We parked in front of the Levee. The kind of bar that didn't have any Yelp reviews and most likely would not turn up in any tourist guides. A row of Harleys lined the street in front of the bar, dripping with rain. They even looked loud.

We entered the bar. The doors squealed on rusty hinges, announcing our presence. It was very dark inside. We stood in the doorway waiting for our eyes to adjust. The jukebox was playing some type of speed punk, rock/rap mashup. The person singing sounded like a monster. The drum beat was impossibly fast. It was some of the worst music I had ever heard. As my eyes finally adjusted to the dark room, I saw hard-looking men and women scattered throughout the bar. The women mostly wore jeans and tank tops. Their arms a gallery of intricate tattoos. The men wore black leather cut-off vests covered in patches. Most had a beer in their hands with plenty more in their bellies. All turned to look at us. The terrible song on the jukebox ended. The bar stood still. It was an old-style jukebox, the type you didn't see much around anymore. The little mechanical arm had to grab the forty-five vinyl record off the turntable, return it back to its sleeve, and fetch another forty-five. The silence in the bar extended for an ungodly amount of time. Someone hacked a smoker's cough and spit right on the ground.

"Bill, maybe we should get out of here," I whispered out of the side of my mouth.

Walton smiled.

"Good afternoon, brothers and sisters!" He ambled towards the bar and I quickly followed in his wake. Finally, the music started again. A cacophony of metal thrashing that sounded indistinguishable from the last song. The bartender was a large man with a large white beard. He looked like Santa Claus's scary cousin, the one who just finished eight to ten years on the federal naughty list.

"Ahoy, drink slinger! I'll have a high alcohol kombucha, please. A bottle of Boochcraft if you have it," Walton roared.

"Mister, we got brown. We got clear. We got beer. No ice. Cash only." Scary Claus leaned his hairy hands on the bar and leered at us.

"Fine. I'll take a glass of your finest IPA." He looked at me. "And a light domestic for my friend here." The bartender reached into a cooler for the two beers. When I grabbed my beer I got the impression the cooler wasn't plugged in. Walton slapped a twenty on the bar.

"For the beer, my good man." Walton leaned in. "And we want to talk to a man named Ike. Let me guess. You never heard of him, right? Well, maybe this will help jog your memory?" Walton pulled another twenty from his jean pocket and started folding it, origami style. What was he doing? This was taking forever. After an insane amount of time Walton finally took the twenty, now folded into an elegant crane (I didn't know he could do that), and placed it on the bar. Scary Santa shrugged.

The bartender smashed the money crane with his fist and made it disappear in his hairy hand. "Shit, you want to talk to Ike? It's your funeral. He's right over there."

We turned to see three men in black battle vests staring at us. The one in the middle was big. Real big. He was smoking a cigar that looked like a cigarette between his fingers. And dangling from his belt, there they were. Two grenades.

This was Ike. He drank from a pitcher of beer like it was a stein. A thick beard streaked with grey cascaded from his cheeks down to his chest. His enormous head was shaved. He had a barrel chest and arms that looked like bags of skin stuffed with boulders.

This was the man that took Abigail. I knew it in my guts, which were currently dancing in my belly. But looking at him, I didn't have a clue how we were going to get her back. One wrong move and Ike would kill her. Certainly. Not to mention us. We weren't safe here. I looked to Walton, hoping the Dancing Bears would lead us out of the bar. They didn't. Apparently the Dancing Bears were leading us directly to the scariest man I'd ever seen.

"Ike!" Walton called out like he was running into an old friend at the farmers market. We ambled over. I tried to look nonchalant while holding my beer. I knew I wasn't pulling it off. I felt every leathery eye in the room following us.

"Ike, let me buy you a drink," Walton said. Ike laughed.

"This is my place. I don't pay for drinks." He turned, smiling to the two cronies standing behind him. One was strikingly good-looking. The other was strikingly not. The first had a strong, movie star jawline and piercing blue eyes. He was tall and broad-shouldered. We had found the man I had mistaken for Kern in the security footage. And standing next to him, I was pretty sure, was the other man who grabbed Abigail. Shorter. Wider. In fact, he looked like a thumb. A thumb with beady eyes and a large Roman nose that looked like it had been broken at least a dozen times.

"You want us to get rid of these guys?" said the thumb. Ike shook him off.

"Naw, Toucan," Ike said. "You and Handsome Billy just chill out."

Handsome Billy. Made sense. I wonder how the thumb became "Toucan." Maybe he liked Froot Loops. Ike went on.

"If NBA MVP, two-time champ, and former sixth man of the year Bill Walton has something to say to me, I'm listening." Ike smirked. Walton smirked back.

"So, you're a hoops fan?" Walton asked.

"Nah. Not anymore. But I played a little ball back in the day." Ike shrugged. "In fact, in my prime, not even you could have stopped me." The bar laughed. They all knew who Walton was.

"Is that a fact?" Walton asked.

"That's a big fact. I would have schooled you, Walton." I relaxed a little. If we kept the mood light, maybe we could get out of there without losing any teeth.

"I doubt that, Ike. I doubt that very much indeed," Walton replied, a little too forcefully. I wanted to kick him. I couldn't believe he was antagonizing this guy. Please just agree with the giant biker!

"I had a sky hook, Walton. The most unguardable shot in basketball. I mastered it. Had it down cold."

"There is only one man in this world who mastered that shot. His name is Kareem Abdul-Jabbar and I'm proud to call him a friend." Ike shook his head.

"Shit. Mine was better than Kareem's."

The bar cheered, egging Ike on. This was definitely his home court and we were the visiting team.

"How dare you. If you took that shot anywhere near me, I'd block it right into the stands." Ike roared, laughing.

"Oh, that's rich," Ike said. "You having an acid flashback, Walton? You losing touch with reality? You can barely walk!"

Ike grabbed a handful of pills that were spilled all over the table. Oxycontin. While covering professional football, I had seen the highly addictive painkiller used in many locker rooms. But I had never seen them gulped like M&Ms by the fistfull. Ike washed the pills down with some beer, a combination that certainly wasn't recommended by his physician.

"Enough, Ike. I have to talk to you about something very important. Is there someplace private we can talk?"

"This is my bar. And we're all friends here. You can tell me anything."

"Okay, Ike, fine. I'm here to discuss what happened at the Smokeshow the other night."

Ike's eyes went wide at the mention of the Smokeshow. Walton had surprised him. It took him a second to regain his composure.

"I don't know what you're talking about. And I think it's time for you to get the fuck out of here, old man."

The malice was carved in Ike's face. Here before us sat a dangerous man. I felt it in my body. It's one thing to know it in your head, intellectually. To acknowledge that you were in a slightly iffy situation and that there was a nonzero chance that you might be seriously hurt. I could handle that. My heart might race, but I could channel the alertness to different what-if scenarios. I could occupy myself by calculating escape routes. But once the fear becomes so tangible and real that the brain is able to shoot its signal of panic down the spine and into the adrenal glands, those glands start to pump adrenaline in the body. Adrenaline makes the heart start beating powerfully, which is good, if you are fighting or running for your life. It gives that extra oomph that might be the difference between life and death. But if one feels that adrenaline spike while trying to stay calm, the shaking starts. I started to feel the rumble. My heart pounding. My hands shook and I spilled beer on my pants.

"I can't just walk away, Ike. You see, you took something that belongs to a very good friend of mine. If you give me what you took, and give it to me safe, I can get you the money. Everyone can walk away happy. I don't care about the money and neither does my friend. We just want…" Walton stopped playing games. "We just want her back safe."

Ike turned around to his two cronies. They were as shocked as he was that Bill Walton knew what they had done.

"Sorry, I don't know what you're talking about, Walton. Wish I could help you," Ike said sarcastically. He couldn't admit he took

Abigail but he wanted us to know he did. He was proud of it.

"Besides, if I had done what you're talking about, hypothetically, there's no fucking way you'd get back shit until I got paid all this money you're talking about."

"Come on, Ike. You want the money, I want the girl safe. Let's work this out. For the love of everything good on this earth."

"Eh," he finally said. "Fuck you. Get out of here."

"Just give us the girl, you dirty grease monkeys," I heard myself say. I meant to think it, but I said it. Must have been the adrenaline surge, the thought gained verbosity and came tumbling out of my mouth. It did not go over well. Ike pulled a huge knife and stabbed it deep into the wood of the table. The knife swayed like an arrow that had just hit its target. Handsome Billy and Toucan leaned in. Recognizing the provocation. The escalation.

"Who the fuck are you, little bald man?"

"Me? I'm Dave Pasch. I do play-by-play..." I said. No reaction. "I've been nominated for a few regional Emmys?"

"Forget about Dave," said Walton. Which was the first time I appreciated hearing him say that. "We're talking about the girl."

"And I'm telling you, you better stop asking questions and get the fuck out of here." Ike chugged the last of his pitcher stein. There was a giant red eyeball tattooed on the back of his hand. It stared at me as he drank. He wiped the beer from his chin and stood up. And, for the first time since we ran into Yao Ming in Houston, I saw Bill Walton look up at someone.

Ike stood about 7'3" and ran a good 350 pounds. Walton sized him up.

"You got a nice frame on you. Where'd you play ball?"

"I averaged twenty and ten for Montana State back in '96." Ike gave a half-smile. "Then I wised up and realized I didn't like working without getting paid."

Walton shook his head.

"Ike, it's called playing basketball, not working basketball. If you don't appreciate the joy of competition and the fierce ecstasy of engaging in battle with the best then you would have made a pretty bad teammate and a very easy opponent."

"College basketball is a racket, man," Ike sneered. "Look at you. You're making money off it. Schools are making money. Coaches are making money. Shoe companies are making money. But nothing for the athletes. That's un-American, man. And they call me a criminal." The bar laughed. They were an easy audience.

"We both got our rackets, Walton. You and me. We're actually a lot alike."

"You're nothing like me," Walton said. "You're a disgrace." Ike's nostrils flared like an ox. His leather creaked.

"I could have wiped the floor with you, Walton. Even in your short ass prime. Guess we'll never know. I'll just have to settle for beating your ass right now, hippie." That got a few "oohs" from the crowd. I felt the electricity in the room rise. The adrenaline had slowed and turned into cortisol in my bloodstream. My vision was tunneling. That's why I didn't notice we had been encircled by Handsome Billy, Toucan, and a dozen other bikers.

"Ike, we don't want to do this." Walton held up his hands. "Where's the girl?"

"Fuck you, Walton. I don't like your questions. I don't like your tone. I don't like your voice. I don't like your face. I don't like your hippie fucking attitude. I don't like you coming into my bar and asking me questions about some shit I don't want to talk about. I'm done talking. I want to 'throw it down' on the hippie."

Ike smiled, revealing gold teeth gleaming in his bearded mouth. Walton, the lunatic, smiled back. I, on the other hand, was not smiling. Looked like I was gonna get my chance to fight after all. Only this fight didn't seem fair.

I remembered Walton's mantra: Preparation. Improvisation. Intimidation.

Okay. Preparation. Prepare for the fight. Over the years, I learned that the difference between winning and losing is not always playing by the rules. The best example that comes to mind is Michael Jordan's push off on Bryon Russell in the 1998 NBA finals. That led to the jump shot that won Jordan his sixth and final championship. No one noticed in the moment. Okay, Bryon Russell and the state of Utah noticed, but no one remembers the push off, everyone just remembers the moment of triumph.

So, I looked around for something to give me an edge. Some kind of advantage. Bars had a lot of things that could be converted into weapons in angry hands. Bottles. Pool cues. Chairs. The problem was, these men were already armed. Knives flashed all around me. I saw Toucan slip on brass knuckles. Oh boy. Preparation was out. Improvisation? I looked around. I saw no Dancing Bears giving me a clue as to what to do next. Intimidation? Check. But I was the one being intimidated. I'm pretty sure I had that backwards.

"Take care of the little bald one," Ike sneered. "Leave Walton to me."

Well, I was about to be beaten. Possibly to death. Should I curl up in the fetal position and beg for mercy? I thought of my wife. Would I see her again? God, how I loved her.

Bikers looked down at me. Too many to count. They shuffled forward, tightening the space. Handsome Billy bluffed a lunge and I flinched. I managed to slide behind Walton. We were back to back. Surrounded. I tasted blood in my mouth. I had bit my tongue at some point. In the distance someone screamed.

Who was it? Was it me? Was I already screaming? No, it wasn't a person. It was a door. The door to the bar had swung open, the rusty hinges screaming. Harsh sunlight backlit the interlopers. The brilliant light busting into the bar must have been the last gasps of daylight. The sun's angle, close to the tree line and the industrial buildings of the surrounding area, lit the bar with magic hour light. Like a photographer's dream. The men blinked and covered their eyes trying to see who was walking in. The doors slammed shut. The sunlight was gone, then replaced with another light. A camera light.

Stephanie. She was holding a microphone, followed by Nick shouldering a camera. She saw us and rushed over.

"And here's Bill Walton mixing it up with some of Washington's biggest college basketball fans. Hello everybody, you're live on the Pac-12 Network!" She said as Nick swung the camera and its 2000 Lux LED light in our direction. The bikers reacted to the camera like vampires fleeing crucifixes.

"Get that camera out of here!" someone yelled as they covered their faces and scattered. The only one to not move was Ike. He was staring at Walton. Walton was returning the favor. Stephanie somehow pushed her way through. I had seen bravery before, but this was remarkable. Two seven-footers who were about to come to blows suddenly had a 5'7" fireball between them with a microphone in her hand.

"Hey, Bill. It looks like none of these guys want to be interviewed. Maybe we should get out of here," Stephanie said. Walton leaned into Ike.

"Where is she?"

"Listen to your little friend, hippie. You should get out of here."

"Where is she?!" Walton screamed.

Ike gave another gold-toothed smile and shrugged. Stephanie pulled on Walton's arm, literally twisting it.

"Bill. Come on, we have a game to do."

Hearing the word "game" snapped Walton out of his stare down with Ike and he allowed himself to be pulled out of the room.

"This ain't over, hippie!" Ike yelled. Stephanie held Nick's belt as he walked backwards, keeping the camera aimed at bikers until we left the bar.

"I'll see you again, Walton!" Ike bellowed as the door squealed shut. "I'll be seeing you again real soon!"

Chapter 17

We piled into the production van, which was parked right outside the bar. Nick drove. Fast. He peeled into the street, gunning the van to the highway.

"Fuck, dudes!" he shrieked. "What the fuck were you guys doing in there? Did you see how big that guy was?!" I checked behind us for Harleys giving chase, but thankfully there were none. Just an old, beat-up car fading in the distance.

"Uh, Stephanie," I said, struggling with my seat belt. "My rental car. We left it back there."

"We'll come back for it, Dave. We gotta go. You two are supposed to be on camera in forty-five minutes and Google Maps is telling me we're an hour away from the arena." Walton turned to her.

"Use Waze. Google tracks your data."

"I don't give a damn about my data, Bill. Did you two happen to remember we have a game tonight?!"

"Of course," Walton said. "We were just wrapping up some business."

"Business?! What business did you have getting in a fight in a biker bar?!"

"Thank you for your help, Stephanie," I said, trying to change to subject. "You come bursting in biker bars with cameras often?"

"Not often, no. I just figured you might need some help and a bar full of criminals probably didn't want to be seen killing you on camera."

Nick hit a turn a little too fast. Something in the back fell over.

"How did you find us?" I asked.

She opened her backpack and took out another photograph from the traffic camera. This time we could see the driver of the van. Well, kinda. Like Toucan and Handsome Billy, he also had a hat pulled down low and a bandanna pulled up high. But you clearly see his hands around the wheel. One of which featured a tattoo of a giant red eyeball. The very same tattoo I had just seen on the back of Ike's hand.

"I tracked the tattoo. If you had let me finish before you two ran off I would have told you that, in addition to the license plate, I found out the driver of the van was the leader of a criminal organization based out of your favorite drinking hole, the Levee."

"That place has warm beer."

"Your big, bearded friend in there has been investigated for just about every crime there is. Drugs, prostitution, human trafficking, kidnapping..." Walton and I exchanged a look. "The list goes on."

"Am I crazy?" Nick asked. "Or did that guy have two grenades on his belt?"

"Relax, Nick. That's how I know he's not tough. Maurice Lucas never had to wear grenades on his belt to intimidate anyone. Maurice Lucas in Bermuda shorts and a pair of flip-flops was more intimidating than Ike could be wearing a dozen grenades around his belt." Walton crossed his arms and looked up. "I miss you, Luke."

For the next half hour Nick drove like a bootlegger with a trunk full of moonshine, pulling a few moves that were highly questionable in their legality. In fact, he started to remind me of another North Carolina native: Richard Petty. Nick celebrated as we pulled into the parking lot of Key Arena.

"Made it! Whoo! Five minutes 'til pre-broadcast. Twenty minutes 'til tipoff!"

"Okay, Nick. Make sure we laid graphics down on all the highlight packs during pre-pro. Have Big John check to make sure the TIF line is open and we are good on the first mile of transmission. Tell everybody we're having a last-minute talent meeting and we'll be right in."

Nick nodded as he memorized his instructions from Stephanie, clicked his seat belt off, and hopped out of the van. I reached for the door. Stephanie locked it.

"Oh, no," she said. "You're not going anywhere. I want answers. Real answers. Beans. It's time to spill them."

"Stephanie, thanks for the help. But let's just do the game and forget what just happened."

Walton unlocked the door, put his fingers in the handle, but Stephanie locked it back down before he could open it.

"Nobody is going anywhere until you two tell me what is happening!"

We stared at each other. The three of us locked in a test of wills and Bill and I weren't going to back down. We couldn't tell Stephanie what we were up to. There were too many ramifications.

"Look, if we don't get there…" She checked her watch. "In four minutes, then who do you think is going to take the blame? The veteran broadcasters or the new producer? So please tell me what the hell is going on so I don't get fired because I'm not leaving this van until you tell me what's happening!"

Walton said nothing.

"Out with it, Walton! All you ever do is talk so start talking! Why do you care about that dirty old van? Why were you in that biker bar?" Stephanie's eyes meant business. "And why did you keep asking that giant biker where the girl was. What girl?"

Bill looked to me. I shrugged. We had a better chance of finding Abigail with Stephanie by our side than with her fighting against us. And I certainly didn't want to see her get fired because we missed the broadcast.

"Okay," he finally said. "What I'm about to tell you stays between the three of us." Stephanie nodded and Bill told her everything that had happened in the past two days in a concise, focused manner in which I didn't know he was capable of communicating. If Stephanie was shocked, she didn't show it. She processed every bit of information, interrupting only to ask a few pointed, pertinent questions. When Walton finished, Stephanie shook her head, amazed.

"Your goddaughter was kidnapped and you two knuckleheads, while calling the Pac-12 Tournament, managed to find the evil biker gang that did it?"

We shrugged.

"Okay," Stephanie nodded. "I want to help."

Walton scoffed. "Absolutely not. Under no circumstances can you be involved in this. Dave and I have this under control!"

"Guys. C'mon, I'm bored out my mind. I can produce college hoops in my sleep. In fact, you get mad if I actually try to do anything!" Walton said nothing. "You're a stubborn old mule, aren't you?"

Walton wasn't budging.

She smiled, then said, "Stubbornness we deprecate, firmness we condone. The former is my neighbor's trait..."

"The latter is my own," Walton finished. He smiled. "John Wooden."

Walton was looking at Stephanie with fresh eyes. He stretched his arms out wide.

"Stephanie, I was totally wrong about you. I offer you my fullest apologies. We are now forever friends. Teammates. Amigos para siempre! There will be no more falsehoods between us." He hugged her. Eventually, she hugged back.

I wasn't invited into the hug. I kind of patted Stephanie on the back.

"Okay, we're a team," Stephanie said, breaking the hug. "And I promise we'll figure out how to get your goddaughter back from Ike, unharmed." She checked her watch again. "But we got ninety seconds to get you on air. What do you say we start off this newfound friendship by not getting me fired?"

Chapter 18

"There's a dribble drive handoff to Mason Thorogood, who turns to the basket and slams it down! Oh, my! Colorado goes up eight with three minutes to go!" I wiped my brow. This game was good.

"Now there is a big man who knows how to throw it down!" Walton thundered. "Let it be known, Mason Thorogood! Shout it from the mountaintops! Remove the safety tag from the mattress! Turn on your hazard lights. The cows are coming home to roost!"

Oregon took the ball, desperate for some quick points.

"Bill, it's another stellar game for Mason Thorogood, the athletic seven-foot Denver native is a surefire top five pick in next year's draft."

"The Oregon Ducks have had no chance to fly against the dominance of Mason Thorogood. Look at that rejection!" Thorogood swatted a layup into the seats. I was surprised Oregon was still trying to score in the lane. Tonight, that was Mason Thorogood's domain. Stephanie threw a replay on the screen in perfect rhythm.

"Look at this! Mason Thorogood doesn't fall for the pump fake. He's too smart, too intelligent. He waits patiently and swats that weak shot outta there! Glorious! Unbelievable!"

"Thorogood is only nineteen years old and some say he's still growing!"

"You never stop growing, Dave. Please. Spiritually. Emotionally. The growth never stops! All human beings, if healthy, should be growing every day with courage and the conviction in our hearts to be better tomorrow than we were today!"

"Yes, of course. But I was talking physically."

"I feel like I've grown today."

"I feel like you have, too, Bill. But not physically." My word. Even on a good night, Bill made it tough to get through a broadcast.

"Mason Thorogood is a perfect example of what Ron Barth should aspire to be."

Great. During this fantastic game, Walton was now talking about a player on a team who wasn't playing.

"Bill is talking about University of Washington big man Ron Barth, who has not been as dominant as some analysts think he should be. There's a lot of talk on Twitter, where people are saying the young artist needs to put down the paintbrush and get in the paint. What do you think, Bill? Can a sensitive artist be aggressive enough to dominate the low post?"

"Please. Pasch! You fool!"

I bristled visibly and gave silent thanks for not being on camera. I hated being called a fool on air, which Walton did all the time.

"Barth can embrace art and basketball," Walton blundered on. "The great artists were Renaissance men. He needs to bring the power of art to his game. You think Vincent van Gogh couldn't dunk a basketball?"

"Bill, I don't think there was basketball in nineteenth-century Holland."

"But if there was, he would have been a powerful guard. The vision! The creativity! Starry night! Sunflowers! Barth can be a painter and dominate the paint. Warrior spirit. Peaceful heart. The Peaceful Warrior!

"Peaceful Warrior?" I asked. "Sounds like an oxymoron."

"That's because your mind is closed! Dave, the two aren't mutually exclusive. Please. In fact, it's imperative they work together as one! Yin and Yang! 'Long distance runner, what are you standing there for? Get up, get out, get out of the door! There's a dragon with matches that's loose on the town, takes a whole pail of water just to cool him down. Fire. Fire on the mountain!' Ron Barth, listen to the immortal lyrics of my great friend Robert Hunter! Become the fire on the mountain." A graphic appeared on our monitors listing great athletes who were also artists. I had to chuckle.

"Bill, look at this terrific graphic from our producer. Jim Thorpe, the greatest multisport athlete of all time, was a charcoal artist. Jim Brown, the unstoppable force for the Cleveland Browns, plays piano and became a tremendous actor when his playing days were done. Serena Williams, possibly the greatest tennis player of all time, paints. And Kobe Bryant, while tragically missing out on the college basketball experience, did win an Oscar for best animated short."

"Oh, my goodness. The artistry! The passion! The skill! Great work, Stephanie! What a job you are doing. Truly fantastic producing!"

Stephanie chimed in our ears, "Thank you, Bill. I appreciate it, but please stop saying my name on air. No one cares."

Thorogood led Colorado to a big win for the Buffaloes, who were headed for the semifinals. The final buzzer sounded and Stephanie ran over to us.

"Great game, guys. You ready to go talk to Ike?"

I suppressed a shudder. "I don't think it's a great idea for us to go walking back into that bar."

"That's just it," Stephanie said with a twinkle in her eye. "Ike's not at the bar."

"Okay. Then where is he?"

Stephanie smiled.

Chapter 19

The knife looked at home in Ike's hand. Like it was a natural extension of his thick, tattooed arms. He raised it high in the air and the little girl screamed. Ike smiled, showing his gold teeth. Then he brought the knife down with a wet thud.

Bill, Stephanie, and I watched Ike cut his daughter's birthday cake through the window of Planet FunZone, an indoor playground where dozens of kids ran around having the time of their lives. They climbed yellow ladders, went down red slides, and played in ball pits that looked like giant bowls of Skittles. And one particularly happy little girl dug into the first piece of her birthday cake.

She was probably around seven. Tiny and adorable. In stark contrast to her giant, ugly father. We went inside. Not rushing. Not in a hurry. But not slow. We looked around, heads on a swivel, walking straight at Ike as he served cake. We got lucky with the angle. His back was to us as we approached. We were counting on the element of surprise.

"Hello, Ike," Walton said. He turned around. His expression migrated from surprise to anger and then back to his natural scowl.

Ike shook his head. Then he kind of laughed. He said quietly to Walton, "Oh man. You just fucked up."

"We just want to talk to you, Ike," Stephanie said. "That's it. Just talk."

"What, no camera this time?" Ike snapped back to Stephanie. "Man, what's wrong with you people? Even the worst psychos know better than to talk business when a man's around his children." Ike handed the knife to another parent. "Hey, Peg, can you finish up for me? I gotta talk to these folks real quick."

Ike led us to the far corner of the room, away from the kids. I noticed he wasn't wearing grenades at his daughter's birthday party. It gave me hope. Somewhere in that giant, scary man was some good sense.

"How the fuck did you know where I was?" He seemed confused and his confusion was making him angrier. He popped a Xanax, holding up the bottle as he dry-swallowed a few pills, explaining he liked "taking the edge off" when he was around his daughters. Painkillers. Anxiety medication. Ike must have great insurance.

He sighed and seemed to soften. "I didn't think I was going to have to kill you, but now... Yeah, I'm definitely gonna kill all three of you." The calmness in which Ike said those words was chilling.

"We don't want any killing, Ike. Look, we know you have Abigail. We know you took her from the Smokeshow two nights ago." Ike chuckled.

"Bullshit, Walton. I don't know who's going around telling these lies about me, but you don't know jack shit."

The three of us had talked beforehand and agreed, for Gibby's sake, to leave him completely out of the conversation. Luckily, we had so much on Ike, it wasn't a problem.

"We got it all on tape, Ike," I said.

I showed him the security footage on my phone. "There are your friends Toucan and Handsome Billy putting Abigail in the van."

Stephanie held up the photographs from the traffic cameras. "And Ike, next time you run a red light after kidnapping a girl, you should put on gloves. That tattoo on your hand makes you real easy to track down."

Ike's face fell. The man had a very bad poker face.

Over the years I had played a lot of poker. The business of sports broadcasting is a traveling business. And travel meant a lot of waiting around. And waiting around meant poker. I had played cards with my broadcasting partners, the crew, referees, coaches, assistants, and the occasional professional athlete. And I won my fair share of pots over the years. In fact, I once took a thousand dollars off Jeff Van Gundy in a memorable game in the back of a cigar shop in New York City. I knew the game. I knew the faces people made when they had good cards and the faces they made when they didn't. We had a royal flush and, looking at Ike's face, he was busted.

"Wasn't supposed to be a camera back there. I know the guy who put in that whole security system. He puts cameras in half the homes and businesses in Seattle. Lucky for me, he's also a cokehead who can't afford his habit. Makes breaking into places a helluva lot easier when you know where the cameras are. Fucker didn't tell me about the one in back. Me and him are gonna have to have a little talk about that."

I was worried we may have just gotten someone killed. I quickly explained, "That's because the manager put it in himself. Nobody knew about that camera, Ike."

Ike shook his head. He popped another Xanax.

"Man, running the red light was dumb. I was jacked up that night. Having fun. Stupid."

"Here's the good news, Ike," Walton said, reassuringly. "We're not going to go to the cops. Or the FBI. Just give Abigail back and I'll get you the money. That's a promise. No one has to get hurt. No one goes to jail. Let's go get her right now and end this. Tomorrow you'll get the money, I swear to you."

Ike watched his daughter go down the huge slide in the middle of the room. She landed and waved to her father, giggling. Ike waved back with both hands.

"Ike, we just want to get a little girl home to her father."

Ike flinched. In that moment Walton had turned Abigail from a thing to a person. Someone's little girl. Just like his. He shook away the thought.

"Fine, Walton. You want the girl? Yeah, I took her. But I don't have her anymore. It was a gig. We were paid five grand to grab her and hand her over. Hell, we were just a taxi service."

I think the Xanax was making Ike say more than he normally would have. I tried to keep him talking.

"Who hired you?"

"I don't fucking know, man. I never even saw his face. Hell, I only talked to him twice. Once on the phone and again when we dropped off the girl. And he never said a damn word. Not really. He and his partner communicated with... like a robot voice."

"Like Siri?"

"Yeah, right. Siri." Ike imitated the automated voice, "Take the money. Leave the girl." He laughed, enjoying his little imitation. Ike was loose as a goose.

"What did they look like, the two men?" Stephanie asked.

"Strong fuckers. Short, but thick. I didn't see much else. They were wearing ski masks and pointing AKs at us. We made it quick."

AK-47s. Those were the same two guns pointed at Abigail's head in the video. I remembered her screams. So disturbing. I tried to imagine her in a better place. I thought about the picture of her hiking in front of Mount Rainier on a beautiful, clear day.

Her Finstagram, I realized. "You knew she was at the Smoke-show because you followed her Finstagram." I was proud of myself for putting that together.

"You mean, her Finsta?"

"Yeah." Damn. "Her Finsta." Whatever.

"Yeah, that's right. When they called us, that robot voice gave us her Finsta handle so we could track her down."

I had wondered if Abigail noticed anyone following her. People lurking in the shadows. Now I realized all you needed to follow someone was social media. And being followed was a good thing. Strange world.

"But that was her private account," Walton explained. "She would have had to accept your friend request."

"I didn't use mine, dipshit," Ike sneered. "We have tons of Finsta accounts from all kinds of people so we can…" Ike stopped himself. "Don't worry about it. Point is: the girl accepted a friend request from someone she thought was another hot girl her age, when in fact it was… me." Ike laughed. He found that hilarious.

I found it disturbing.

A woman marched up to Ike. She had to be the mother of Ike's daughters; they all had the same oval faces and light blonde hair. She was also clearly one of the few people on the planet Ike didn't intimidate.

"Hey, ding dong, we only have the place for ten more minutes. Think you can spend two seconds with your daughters? You won't see them again for a month." It was fun seeing Ike put in his place. "And give me some money to tip the waitress."

Ike took out a roll of money the size of a grapefruit. He casually peeled off a few hundreds and handed them to the former Mrs. Ike. That was some tip.

"Okay, shitbirds. I've answered all your questions. Now get the fuck out of here. Walton, a little piece of advice. If I see you again, I'm gonna beat your ass. That's a promise."

"Ike, I abhor violence in all forms. Fighting is a waste of precious energy. What would we gain by trading blows?! Fanning the flames of our primitive egos? I've won two NBA championships and two NCAA titles! Please! My ego is fine!"

"You don't want to fight, hippie? That's fine with me. Just don't ever let me see you again."

Ike turned his back on us. He walked over to the birthday girl, who leapt into his arms, laughing. He tossed her in the air with a look of pure joy that seemed out of place on the hard man's face.

Chapter 20

I drove the production van south on the 405 as we headed back to the Levee to pick up my rental car. The van handled like a cruise ship but I couldn't help but appreciate the sheer size and weight of the vehicle. Stephanie and Bill stretched out in the back, each taking their own row of the bench seating.

Thirty minutes later we came to a stop in front of the Levee. I didn't see my rental car. Or, as I quickly came to realize, I just didn't recognize it. My Chrysler 300 was trashed. The driver side window was punched out. All that remained of the windows were pieces of glass scattered like worthless jewels on the ground. The roof was concave, like someone had jumped on it. The back bumper was half bent, loose, and hanging off the back right side of the car. It looked like someone had tried to kick it off, and almost succeeded, then decided that half-off was funnier, so they left it like that.

We got out of the van and walked around the car as Stephanie apologized. "I'm sorry, Dave. I guess I should have let you drive it back?"

The car was covered in graffiti. Words like "DIE HIPPIE," "WALTON SUX," and "FUCK U WALTON" were written in dripping red spray paint. We circled around to the other side of the car.

"Oh, Dave. They spray-painted male genitalia all over your car."

"I think they are middle fingers," I said, hopefully.

"Okay," Walton said. "You can think whatever you want." Whether they were genitalia or middle fingers, the point was the same. Walton put his hand on the relatively undamaged hood of the car and touched his other hand to his heart.

"Long may she run, Dave," Walton said. "Long may she run."

Damn it. I loved that car.

"Look on the bright side, Dave," Stephanie said. "At least none of the graffiti is about you."

To be honest, that was the part that bothered me the most. Sure, it sucked to have my rental car trashed. But once again I was completely ignored and it was all about Walton. They couldn't have taken a moment to spray-paint one thing about me? I would have been happy with a single, "Screw you bald guy!" That honestly would have made me feel better. But as always, next to Bill Walton, it was like I didn't exist.

I got in the car and pushed the ignition. It started. At least it was still running. Stephanie got behind the wheel of the van.

"Be safe in that thing. See you back at the hotel." She said as she took off, laughing.

The inside of the car was just as wrecked. But the stereo was still there. Unfortunately for me. Walton turned it on. Guess which station? Of course, it was the Sirius/XM Grateful Dead Channel. I'm not sure he listened to anything else.

The driving, droning beat that could only be one of about a million Grateful Dead songs assaulted my ears.

"Maybe a little Jerry will help you out," Bill said, smiling. I did not smile.

"No, actually. It won't. Walton, please. I can't listen to the Dead right now."

"What are you talking about? You love the Dead!"

"No, you do, Bill! You do! You listen to them all day, every day, and I just can't stand it anymore. Not now. My God, it's all so repetitive!"

"Repetitive?! No! No two songs are the same! No two notes are the same! Endless originality! Spontaneous creation!"

"No, no, no, no. I can't. Not tonight. One night. One night! We are not going to listen to the damn Grateful Dead!"

I smashed the radio off with my finger.

"I went to 854 Grateful Dead shows and no two were the same."

"Bill!"

"I'm just saying they are not repetitive," he said quietly and pouted in the passenger seat as we drove in silence. The rare quiet was nice, but that meant I could clearly hear the glass rattling around the back seat like a thousand broken teacups. It seemed to get louder with every turn of the wheel. I looked over to Walton. He looked like a giant golden retriever who lost his favorite tennis ball. Was he crying?

"Fine, turn it back on," I groaned.

Walton smiled as he turned the music back on. He took huge sniffs of the air, like a giant, red grizzly.

"You smell that?" Walton asked.

"Nope," I lied.

"Smells like the scoundrels used the back seat for a toilet."

Twenty minutes and half a song later we were back on University Way, passing the neon signs and sidewalks full of kids out and about on a Thursday night. We slowed down in front of the Smokeshow and, sure enough, Cal was gone. There were new bouncers working the front door, very professionally checking each and every ID. We drove on. At least we had done some good in the past two days.

Chapter 21

I don't like to use the phrase "I need a drink." I think it espouses a kind of casual alcoholism, a running away from our problems and escaping down a bottle of forget-juice. I tended to think that it only makes problems worse and things don't really get better until you dry up and have a conversation between your heart and the man upstairs. But in this case, I needed a gosh darn drink.

We found Stephanie at the hotel bar. She waved us over to a booth in the back, away from the crowd. An elderly waiter came over and I ordered a very tall Pinot Gris. Stephanie had a double Buffalo Trace, neat. Walton asked for high alcohol kombucha but reluctantly settled for an Elysian microbrew.

"Okay," Stephanie said. "So Ike took her but doesn't have her. What now?"

"I don't know," I said. "We're at a dead end."

"All right. I came into this late," Stephanie said. "Tell me everything that happened. Start at the beginning."

"Two nights ago Walton's old teammate Phil Engels approaches us after the game. He tells us his daughter has been kidnapped. He got a video from the people who took her."

We showed Stephanie the video. Once again, it was horrible. And she agreed with Sara Soho's opinion that it was taken on a boat. She also agreed that gave us very little to go on.

"They said no cops but that could clearly just be a bluff, right?" Stephanie asked.

"Agreed. But not worth the risk," Walton answered. "The kidnappers gave Phil three days to put together ten million dollars."

"Wow. And he can do that? He's got that kind of money?"

"Yes. He's a pharmacist."

"He's in pharmaceuticals, Bill."

"Same! Same!"

"Okay, how did he get this video? Who sent it?"

"It was a text from his daughter's phone," I explained. "Phil tried to call back but the phone was turned off. Find My Phone didn't work. Which doesn't necessarily mean anything. It's either turned off, out of juice, or out of range."

Stephanie nodded.

"Dead end number one."

The old waiter brought our drinks. We ordered some food, not even looking at the menu. Three burgers. Two meat, one veggie. After the waiter shuffled out of earshot, which wasn't far, I continued.

"Then we talked to Kaitlin Bustamonte, Abigail's roommate. They went out together to the Smokeshow, where Abigail was kidnapped. A kidnapping that was recorded on a secret security camera. I went through all the footage from that night, from all the cameras, and didn't find anything else. Well, I thought I had found a suspect in Abigail's ex-boyfriend, Kern—"

"What was Kern's last name?" Stephanie asked as she jotted down neat, copious notes in her purple binder.

"We never found out. All we know is Kern is his second-middle name."

"Okay. Not helpful. Go on."

"But Kern couldn't have done it. He was in police custody at the time of the kidnapping. A fact I confirmed with a call to the local police, posing as Kern's father."

"Pasch! I'm shocked and proud! Fight the system! Never tell the truth to the cops!"

"Whatever, Bill. Then, with the help of our amazing new producer, we traced the van used in the kidnapping to Guy Gibby, a huge Bill Walton fan, who sent us to the Levee to meet Ike, Seattle's seven-foot-tall Tony Soprano. And we find out he's not a good giant person like Walton. He's a bad giant person."

"Dave, good and evil are constructs. It's yin-yang! One wouldn't exist without the other. The dark has some light, and the light has some dark!"

"Again." I gestured at Stephanie. "Thanks to you we track Ike down at his daughter's birthday party."

"By the way," Walton asked. "How did you know he was going to be there?"

"Simple. I'm a parent."

"Explain."

"My government source searched the Interpol database for convicted criminals with a tattoo of a big red eyeball on their right hand. He hit the jackpot. I got Ike's record with his long, sordid criminal history. The information was a gold mine. It had everything. His address. His ex-wife's address. The names of his kids and their birthdays, one of which just so happened to be today. Her seventh. I have a daughter and I know the kind of places seven-year-old girls like to go on their birthday. I called around and there was a reservation at Planet FunZone under a one Mister Isaac Jacobs."

"Who's that?" Walton asked.

"It's Ike, Bill," I said, gently.

"Oh, of course. Ike is short for Isaac! Such a proud biblical name, sullied by a pathetic excuse of a human being!"

"Great job, Stephanie. But who is this 'friend in the government' giving you all this great information?" I asked.

"A good reporter never reveals her sources," she said with wink. "I still have some journalistic integrity."

"Okay, I respect that. But let's get back to Abigail," I said. "Ike took her and handed her off to two short, thick dudes in ski masks with AK-47s."

"Unless Ike is lying?" Stephanie offered.

"I believed him," I replied. "He was too doped up to lie that well. As far as I can tell, Ike doesn't have many weaknesses but I know he has at least one: a very bad poker face."

"And here we are, back at square one," Walton sighed. "A dead end. A very ungrateful dead end."

Everyone was quiet. Another waiter, who I couldn't believe was even older than the first, brought over our food. The Hyatt House knew what they were doing. The buns were brioche and perfectly toasted. The burger was served open face with a pile of fresh, carefully arranged onion, lettuce, and tomato skewered with a long bamboo pick. The fries were a masterpiece. Steaming, thick cut, perfectly seasoned, and piled next to ramekins of ketchup and mayonnaise. I removed my onion, added the ketchup, saving my mayonnaise for the fries, and attacked my burger. I didn't realize how hungry I was. It had been a very long day. After a few ravenous bites I came up for air. Looking over, I noticed Stephanie was matching me bite for bite but Bill hadn't touched his food.

"Something wrong with the veggie burger, Bill?"

"Is there nothing else we can do? Something we missed? Is there not a single thread to be pulled? A rock to be turned over?"

We thought. We thought long and hard. The answer was no. We had nothing.

"Maybe it's time to go to the cops?" I asked.

Walton bristled. "No. I know what I have to do. Something I was saving as a last resort." Walton stood up, pushing away his untouched veggie burger.

"Okay, where are we going?" Stephanie asked, wiping her mouth and grabbing her backpack. Walton shook his head.

"Sorry," he said, looking at us. "On this mission, I go alone."

Chapter 22

I didn't sleep much that night and what little sleep I had was peppered by nightmares. Men. Guns. Screaming. I decided to stop wrestling with the pillow and got out of bed. I showered, dressed, and by 6 A.M. I was in the hotel restaurant pulling the tab down on a vat of coffee. Seattle's Best was the brand of the coffee, which annoyed me for no reason.

We had a game at noon, but I obviously had more on my mind than the upcoming contest between the Universities of Washington and Colorado. I shoveled down my continental breakfast and was slurping my second cup of Seattle's "Best" when Walton walked in from outside. He was wide-eyed, peaceful, and covered in leaves. It looked like he hadn't slept. He strolled over to the beverage station and helped himself to a couple of tall apple juices.

"Bill, good morning. Are you okay?" I asked. He flashed a thumbs-up as he dropped off the juices and ordered an omelet from a stern-faced man in a white chef hat. No words were spoken. He just pointed at the various ingredients he wanted, which appeared to be most of them. Then he stayed there watching the man make his omelet. When it was done, Walton walked around and gave the omelet chef a long hug.

By the time Bill sat down with his omelet, Stephanie, fresh from the hotel gym, had sat down with a cup of coffee. Walton ate his omelet with reverence. Each bite was like a sacrament. Dissolved on the tongue, not chewed.

"So, guys," Stephanie said. "I was thinking. If all we know is she was taken on a boat at some point, before our game today we should start canvassing the fishing docks around the city."

Walton held a finger up. He paused his slow meticulous eating process to dig a bunch of crumpled napkins out of his pockets. Each pocket seemed to contain a few more. Finally, he handed them all to me in a pile.

I looked at the napkins. He had written on them. I tried to put them in order, but there didn't seem to be an order that made sense to me. Then I noticed symbols in the corners that seemed to hint at a pattern. It didn't read from right to left, or up and down... it was more like the cube from the alien language in the movie *Contact*, with Jodie Foster. One of my family's favorite movies.

"Bill, what happened last night? Where did you go?" Stephanie asked. Bill drank his second apple juice, then he tapped the napkins with a carrot-sized index finger.

We looked at the napkins. I think I had put them in order, according to the symbols.

"Bill, what is this?" Stephanie asked. Walton didn't answer. He quietly ate his omelet, smiling at every bite. Stephanie and I shrugged to each other and began to read.

Chapter 23

(The following was written by Bill Walton.
All spelling and punctuation are his.)

(Napkin 1)

I left the hotel and wandered, but not all those who wander are lost... and not all those who were lost can be found. But everything that should be found is to be found. And found post haste! But search we must and seek we can and sometimes what we are seeking for is also searching for us. AHHHHHHHH!! The journey must begin. To where? FINARRIO!

(Napkin 2)

The bus! The city bus! How I love it so!! Where are we going, Johnny? All the way. ALL the WAY. To the end of the line. To the twilight time. Just enough light, just enough, I could search the farm old reliable. The McTotts Family Farm. Oh, I knew it well. Had it changed? All things must. The only constant. Change. My old friend. And yet, I knew. I KNEW. (Faith?) that it must be. There must still be a little bit of magic in that old top hat. That old top hat he found.

(Napkin 3)

I knew what I was looking for. The secret of the universe. KNOW what you want! Yes imagine it! See it in your mind! Smell it with your mind nose! Old farmer McTotts. He of early bedtimes he didn't know. For here is the place where they grow. Water. Sun. What's cooking in that field? Cow pies. Here in the groves of pine near the edge of the fence was the dark growing place. It had been years. Decades? Since I had walked this farm searching for the grail. The holy Psilocybin. My old friend. You trickster! Brother Coyote. On your footsteps, I reach. Like a somnambulist truffle pig I wandered. Or was guided?????????????? _{Jerry.} 'Til I found them, oh yes, I found them, and as the moon rose I consumed. Or was consumed....

(Napkin 4)

My little fungi friends were not hard to find. The dancing bears took me there. I ate them slow. Earth! I ate them as the earth will one day eat me. Eat me! Fractal cycles in time, time, time. TIME. In the darkness of a grove of weeping willows. I ate, ate, ate. 8. The number 8 sideways. THE INFINITE. IN-FINITE! The show never ends! The tour must go on! O WIDE WORLD WHAT SECRETS DO YOU CONTAIN? WHAT LIES UNDER YOUR FOLDS! YOUR CREVASSES! WHAT DARKNESS! Where are the cracks between the cracks? The places where the light becomes the dirt. Holes! The world full of holes. Holes of the holy. Holes are the WHOLE. The graves of the great! Dancing like the pyramids. Not moving but moving. Chaotic stillness for 10 thousand years! Yet the sun is not spinning it is shining. Inner light! The sun my heart! My head the moon! Unrequited love. In between heaven and earth I live. Purgatory! Ancient ills, how to mend? How to heal? Jerry! I need you now!

(Napkin 5)

Bobby Weir! Mickey Hart! Phil Lesh! Pig Pen! I used my phone for light. Thank you, Steve Jobs! True genius cannot be stifled. True genius rises with the power of dawn. The power of the Missoula flood! One thousand glaciers, vaporized! In an instant! Fill your eyes with the shafts of light emerging from the holes where shadows live! Multitudes surely. REBOUNDS! Make the misses into makes! Desire! The intangibles can never be tangible! Never! The painted area. The mud like paint! The paint that covers the earth. Red, always red. Why? Blood magic? To my knees! To my knees, I fell! To my knees, I feel! I feel on my knees the powers, the four corners. Brother wolf. Sister crow! The canvas of the world. The art of living! Footsteps of the Gods, and yet nothing. Always nothing. Chaos, a river I need to cross. I can make it. I can't make it! I NEED HELP. From the wellspring of my soul that I sing the cry of assistance! I turn to my bench and cry, who are you? Turn to my coach and say, put me in! But we need help and we are humbled. Oh, how we are humbled. Isengard rides on Rohan! We need help! Hear my cries! Help me to find the truth! (Illegible here)

(Napkin 6)

We were up against the wall. An end that could lead us to the end. Where do you find the end of the labyrinth? The one labyrinth, the one maze, the one quest, the one mystery. Where? To the end of the rainbow. Outside is Inside. Inside/inside/outside.

INSIDE OUTSIDE

OUTSIDE INSIDE

POST PERIMETER

OUTSIDE INSIDE

(This is repeated for the whole napkin 6 along with some drawings that look like basketball plays, mostly high post stuff.)

(Napkin 7)

My mentor, my mama... Earth! Hold my feet O forest floor! I needed to run under the moon. To cry in your bosom! O whistling wind! O fiery sun! O Columbia! Mississippi of the West. Rushing waters running, running, hustling back on defense! Always to the sea to the sea to the sea and yet not separate from! We must defend her from the fast break of pollution! Transitional times. TRANSITION D! Banish effort! Effortless effort! The flow always flows! The water drop need not think! I need not either! It acts! It plays! Mickey Hart! Bob Weir! Phil Lesh! Jerrrrryyyyyyyyyyyyyyy!!!

(The rest of the napkin is a crude drawing of Jerry Garcia in the middle of dancing bears.)

(Napkin 8)

Weeping willow tree! Cradle me! Gautama Siddhartha! The bodhi tree. But I am not the buddha. I am not a buddha. I am a bruddah. Barely a man. So many tears! So much wasted time! I gazed at the willows and like them I did cry. Bitter anger! Tragic mistakes. Dire consequences. But what way forth? Forward. Always forward! Courage! Courage! The only currency the universe accepts is courage! Courage! The courage to L O V E

No ideology! No language! Nothing but the real. The promise of the real. NEIL THE REAL. HEART OF GOLD. FEEL THE REAL. BLOCK THE SHOT.

Pure signal now. Fading. Flashing like a strobe. Fading. Fading. Fading.

(Napkin 9)

The final napkin was a strange, beautiful drawing of a coiled snake-like creature wrapping itself around a wineglass. And below the drawing were the words:

END DOWNLOAD

Chapter 24

I carefully put down the last napkin; it was almost falling apart as if it had gotten wet from rain or Walton's tears.

"Bill, what does this mean?" Stephanie asked. "Where did you go last night?"

Bill gently cleared his throat and finally spoke.

"Stephanie, where I went was nowhere, yet everywhere. A place I was able to meaningfully communicate with my ancestors. Not with words, mind you, this was a powerful alchemical connection. And when I say 'my ancestors,' I don't mean my relatives, I mean the ancestors of the universe. The council of the great tribe called humanity."

I rolled my eyes. This was classic Walton. Sometimes I think he said this stuff because it annoyed me so much. Stephanie picked up the last napkin.

"What about the drawing, Bill? What is it?"

"I know nothing of what's on those napkins," Bill explained. "I was in a trancelike state. I was channeling words from a higher realm and that channel is now closed. What's on those napkins is as much a mystery to me as it is to you."

I was furious. "Bill, last night you went into a farmer's field and took mushrooms?!"

"Yes."

I rolled my eyes even further back in my head. Any more and I'd be able to see the back of my skull.

"I thought it would help."

"Huh," Stephanie said. "So this all came from your subconscious. Interesting."

I did a double take. "Stephanie, how in the world could that nonsense be interesting? It's the deluded rantings of a man on drugs."

"Plants," said Walton. "I was on plants, Dave."

"Plants that happen to be a Schedule 1 drug. Thanks a lot, Bill. This was incredibly helpful," I said, sarcastically. "Now, I agree with Stephanie. Our only lead is the fact we know Abigail was taken away on a boat—"

"Wait," Stephanie interrupted. "Bill, your hallucination, experience. Or journey, whatever. I mean, I'm sorry, I don't want to dismiss it."

"Stephanie, you can definitely dismiss it."

"I wouldn't be so sure, Dave."

Stephanie paused, gathering her thoughts.

"Let me tell you guys a story about Captain Woody Pengelly. The F-18 he co-piloted crashed in Afghanistan during a sandstorm and he and his pilot, Lieutenant Colonel Gerald Chu, were captured by Taliban forces. They were kept and tortured for over a year until our government was able arrange a prisoner swap."

Bill and I were silent. Stephanie had our full attention.

"The only problem was, Captain Pengelly came back alone. They kept Lieutenant Colonel Cho. Special Forces wanted to go in and rescue him, but Woody couldn't remember anything about what happened or where they were kept. The doctors and psychologists tried everything they could to get him to remember something, any clue, but he had complete amnesia from the moment they ejected to the moment he woke up in the military hospital. Captain Pengelly was honorably discharged and he went home to Wisconsin."

Stephanie took a sip of her coffee and continued.

"Months later, a few of his buddies took him camping and they brought along some magic mushrooms. He ate a few and in the middle of his trip, or experience or whatever you want to call it…"

"Journey," Walton chimed.

"In the middle of his journey, Captain Pengelly suddenly had a moment of clarity. His deep subconsciousness, where his brain had locked up that experience, suddenly opened. He remembered everything that happened to him in almost photographic detail and, after writing everything down… on napkins… the military was able to track down the Taliban cell and successfully rescued Lieutenant Colonel Cho."

"Oh yeah," I said. "I remember hearing about that."

"Yeah. Needless to say, you didn't hear how Captain Pengelly's memory was jogged. Those details were not released to the public. But, it happened. Thanks to a mushroom journey, a man's life was saved."

I refused to look at Bill, who looked down at me with a grin I could feel.

"Okay, fine," I said. "Maybe there's something here." We looked back through the napkins. Stephanie grabbed the last napkin, napkin nine, the drawing of a snake wrapping itself around a wineglass.

"Phil Engels," she said. "Of course."

"What?" I asked. Stephanie leaned forward. She was excited.

"The subconscious doesn't communicate with words. It uses symbols. If we look at this subconsciously, that is to say, symbolically... The glass next to the snake. What does that remind you of?"

"A snake drinking from a wineglass? I had a Pinot last night. Am I the snake, Bill?"

"You could be, I don't know, Dave! The channel is closed!"

I looked at the picture. A snake wrapped around a wineglass. How was this supposed to help us find Abigail?

"The Bowl of Hygeia!"

Bill and I stared at Stephanie.

"Did you two ever take a mythology class? It's not a wineglass, it's a chalice. A snake wrapped around a chalice, one of the oldest symbols for a pharmacy."

"So?" Bill asked.

"So, Phil Engels." I couldn't believe it, but I realized where Stephanie was going. "He's in pharmaceuticals, right? Bill, I think your subconscious might be suspicious of Phil Engels in a way your conscious mind refuses to be."

"That's absurd," Walton said. "Phil Engels has been a dear friend since the day we met. He was a walk-on at UCLA. Didn't play much but he was one of the most beloved guys on the team! And he helped me out tremendously. I'm not sure if you know this, Stephanie, but I struggled with a serious stuttering problem for most of my life.

It was really bad in college. Everyone would always cut me off, to finish what I was trying to say, thinking they were helping me. Phil, whose sister had a stutter, was the only one who didn't. He worked with me, taught me tricks and relaxation techniques to help me conquer my stutter. I trust him. I love him! I wouldn't be a broadcaster today without the help of Phil Engels. Now you're telling me he kidnapped his own daughter? Preposterous!"

"No, Bill. I'm not saying that," Stephanie said gently. "All I know is deep in your subconscious, your brain wants us to take a closer look at Phil Engels and I say we do."

"You think that's what my subconscious was talking about? In my journey?" Walton asked. She shrugged. I put my arm on his shoulder.

"It's worth a shot, Bill. We have nothing else to go on."

"So be it."

Stephanie nodded. "Okay, we don't have much time. I'm gonna have to skip this afternoon's game to work on this. Are you guys cool doing the game kinda fast and loose without any support from the truck?"

I frowned. Bill smiled.

Chapter 25

"Hitchcock brings the ball up, looking to initiate the offense. Bounce pass to Barth in the low block. Barth turns, puts it on the floor, and dunks it hard! My goodness!"

"Finally!" Walton exclaimed. "The big man throws it down!"

"And he didn't throw it down on just anyone, Bill. Barth threw it down on Mason Thorogood, the best big man in the country! In Washington's first possession of the tournament semifinal, the big Kiwi shows he is not afraid of the one-and-done future lottery pick."

This was a game Ron Barth would remember for the rest of his life. He was like a new man. Unrecognizable from the player we had seen thus far. Colorado wilted under the constant, unrelenting barrage of dunks, rebounds, and blocked shots, courtesy of Ron Barth. In the middle of the second half, Thorogood fouled out of the game with seven points, no rebounds, and may have dropped a few spots in the upcoming draft. The game was a blowout but, with a few minutes left to go, nobody could call this garbage time. A performance this dominating was a pleasure to behold.

"Hitchcock's shot is off but, of course, Barth collects the rebound, steps towards the basket and... wow! What a dunk! How is the basket still standing?!"

"From the hills of New Zealand, and its coasts and volcanoes, across the mighty Pacific Ocean to the other side of the ring of fire, to here in the great Pacific Northwest, Ron Barth is bursting through with the force of Mount St. Helens. Turning peaceful rivers to boiling hot tsunamis of mud. Oh, the humanity!"

"Of course, we don't want to make light of the 1980 Mount St. Helens eruption, Bill, a lot of people died in that horrible tragedy."

"And we weep for them. As we weep in joy seeing what a journey this young man, Ron Barth, has completed. Oh my goodness, what a game."

"Barth, now with thirty-two points, twenty rebounds, and eleven blocked shots. A mighty triple-double."

"Barth has painted a masterpiece. This performance should hang in the Louvre. The power of van Gogh! The grace of da Vinci! Caravaggio! What a game! What a life!"

A terrified Nick, filling in for Stephanie, shouted in our ears. "Uhh, guys, we, uh, got a um, billboard coming up. Mr. Pasch, do you wanna, do you want me to set you up? Or… Here it is!"

I leaned in but Walton shook me off. He was actually taking this billboard himself. The graphic came up and Walton proudly made Ron Barth the Leonard's Lemonade player of the game.

"Congratulations, Ron Barth!" Walton proudly shouted to the heavens. "Who's had a game as strong and powerful as that Leonard's Lemonade taste. Wow! Dave, that is some lemonade. I love this game. I love Ron Barth. I love my job. And I love Leonard's Lemonade."

I couldn't believe it. Ron Barth. Bill Walton. That day, I saw two giant men change before my very eyes. Bill went on.

"Ron Barth, on this proud day you've transformed from docile caterpillar to a tremendous, dunking butterfly who controls the paint and the canvas with equal aplomb and vivacity. I say to you, in your native tongue, that of the proud Maori, Kia ora, Ron Barth. Kia ora."

"Uh-huh. And what does that mean, Bill?"

"Kia ora means hello."

"So, at the end of your long speech to Barth, you just said hello?"

"No, well, yes, but it means so much more than just 'hello.' Pasch, please! It means 'Have life! Be well! Be healthy!' And this is what I wish for this young man. Kia ora. Hello. Have life. Be healthy."

The rest of the game went pretty smoothly as far as Walton was concerned and Nick held it together more or less in the truck. But Bill and I missed having Stephanie in our ear, keeping us in line and headed in the right direction. We survived this game, but doing another one without her wasn't something we'd want to do again. She was one of us now. We were a team.

The game was an unexpected blowout. Barth walloped one last thunderous dunk before his coach pulled him out of the game for his ovation, which he got. Barth walked by the announcer's table and Walton cried out to him.

"Way to throw it down, Big Man!"

Barth stopped. Turned. Met eyes with Walton.

"Cheers, bro. Just call me the Peaceful Warrior from now on. Yeah, I heard what you said about me. Thanks, bro. It helped heaps." Barth smiled gently. The peaceful artist combined perfectly with the warrior we had just seen dominate the game.

"The Peaceful Warrior, Ron Barth, making his exit to deafening applause!" Walton said as Barth was mobbed by his coaches and teammates. A few minutes later the horn sounded and Colorado was put out of its misery. This was definitely the type of game when people hung around afterwards. I'm not sure they'd ever peel Barth off the court. When we left we saw him and Stanford grad Brook Lopez chatting it up. We made a fast exit to our dressing room. Bill was focused. He didn't even stop to insult the refs and, honestly, it looked like it hurt their feelings.

Bill looked at his phone. He had about twenty missed calls and about the same amount of texts from Phil Engels.

"Something's up," Walton said. "I'm gonna call him."

We closed the door to our dressing room and used speakerphone so I could hear. Phil picked up on the first ring.

"Bill! Where have you been?! They sent me instructions for the drop. But something… something's wrong."

"Phil, we're coming over there right now. Just hang tight. Everything is going to be okay." Walton hung up as I raised my own phone to call Stephanie.

"I found something," she said. "A lot of something. I need a little more time. Meet me back at the hotel bar in an hour."

We took the Kia Sorento that Hertz had exchanged for my defiled Chrysler 300. The Sorento was nice, well appointed. Bigger, which was better for Walton, but I missed the Detroit muscle of the 300.

The rain-slicked Seattle streets shimmered in the moonlight as Bill directed me over the I-80 bridge onto Mercer Island, one of the fanciest neighborhoods in one of the most expensive cities in the world. Even the street signs were fancy. I turned down a private, one-lane road next to a few mailboxes, kept left at a couple of forks that led off to neighbor's houses, and eventually arrived at the Engels' gate. I punched in the four digit code Phil texted us and the gate slid open.

We parked in front of the house. Well, it wasn't a house. It was an estate. It was huge. Palatial. There was a fountain made of old stone before the grand entrance. Phil opened the door before we started knocking. He was a wreck. He was wearing the same outfit he was in when I met him. But it no longer said "success." Now his wrinkled, stained clothes said "scared, desperate parent of a missing child." Helen arrived at his side, looking as desperate and terrified as Phil.

"Come in. Come in," they said. I stifled the urge to say "nice place." Now was not the time for compliments. They led us into a dining room that had been converted into a kind of war room. Phil had written every piece of pertinent information on a whiteboard leaned against the wall. Coffee mugs were everywhere. Phil and Helen looked like they hadn't slept for days.

"Look at this." Phil handed Bill his phone and stormed out of the room. Bill held the phone low, so we could both read the text they had received from Abigail's phone.

> PUT THE MONEY IN THE TRUNK OF YOUR CAR AND
> DRIVE TO THE WEST POINT LIGHTHOUSE AT 1 AM.
> PARK THE CAR AND LEAVE THE KEYS AND MONEY
> IN THE CAR. WALK EAST TO FORT LAWN CEMETERY
> AND WE WILL CALL YOU WITH FURTHER INSTRUC-
> TIONS. IF THE MONEY IS TRACEABLE, TRACKED OR
> CONTAINS DYE PACKS, SHE DIES.

"Why didn't they send another video?" Helen demanded.

It was a good question. I thought the same thing. I couldn't tell which was more terrifying. Abigail screaming at gunpoint, or her complete absence. Why not show her this time? Show that they still had her. That she was okay. Maybe she wasn't okay. My heart sank. Phil came back into the room holding a Sig Sauer, a gun carried by cops and soldiers all over the world and now being held in the shaking hand of a desperate father.

"Whoa!" Bill shouted. "Phil, what are you doing with a gun?! Put that down!"

"I'm going to kill them, Bill! I know that area. I'm going to drop off the car by the lighthouse, walk towards the cemetery, and then double back. The second they come for the money, I'm going to grab them and make them take me to Abigail! And then I'm gonna kill them!"

"No, Phil! You can't do this!" Bill turned to Helen. "Please, talk some sense into him!"

"I'm the one who gave him the gun!" Helen shouted back. "It was my father's. It's been in a box in the basement since he died. We have to do something, Bill! We're going to hurt them for what they've done to our baby!"

"When did your father die?" I asked.

Everyone looked at me incredulously.

"What the hell does that have to do with anything?"

"Ten years ago," Helen answered. "My father died ten years ago. Are you happy?!"

"I'm sorry," I said gently. "But if that gun has been in a box in the basement for ten years, it's very likely it will misfire, or not fire at all.

And you'll be killed by trained men with well-oiled machine guns."

There was a beat of silence as my words resonated. They couldn't argue with logic. Logic I had apparently abandoned with my next sentence.

"Let us take care of this," I said. "Bill and I will do the drop."

Walton looked at me, stunned. I continued.

"We'll bring Abigail back safe. I promise. But let us do it. When this is all over, Abigail will need her parents, not two murderers. Or corpses."

The room was silent for an eternity. Finally, Phil sat down. As he did, he dropped the gun to the floor, put his head in his hands, and started crying. Huge sobs that seemed to have been building inside him for days.

"I'm sorry, what's your name?" Helen asked.

"Dave. Dave Pasch. I'm Bill's broadcasting partner."

"I'm sorry, Dave. You're right. You're absolutely right. The last few days have been hell. Get Abigail home. Please. Give those bastards their damn money and bring our baby home."

She nodded at two leather bags sitting under the table. The money. I quickly did the math. A note of any U.S. currency weighs one gram. There are 454 grams in a pound. Ten million dollars in hundred dollar bills would be two hundred and twenty pounds. Split into two bags, a hundred and ten pounds each. Heavy. Manageable, but heavy.

We all stared at the money in front of us.

"I trust you with her life," Phil wept. "More than I trust myself."

Walton walked over and wrapped his two old friends in an immense hug. It didn't seem like my place to join them, so I grabbed the money and headed for the door, leaving them to their moment. Bill joined me outside and helped me put the bags in the trunk of the car. As we pulled away from the estate, Phil and Helen watched us from the doorway. I was hoping by the end of the night their family would be whole. Reunited and ready to start the healing process.

We drove in silence. Walton didn't even put the radio on. Driving around with ten million dollars was terrifying. The power of it. I could feel it. It was just paper. Men have killed and died for far less than we had in the trunk. Life for paper. What a trade. The silence was broken by a call from Stephanie.

"Where are you guys?"

"Sorry," I said on the car's speakerphone. "That took longer than we thought. We have the money. We're doing the drop at one in the morning. Did you come up with anything?"

"Yeah, I think I found some suspects."

"How many?"

"About half a million."

Chapter 26

I valeted the Sorento. Walton declined the bellhop's offer to assist with our bags and carried them to the hotel bar. It was Friday afternoon and starting to get busy. People were everywhere. The hotel had security. All things considered, the ten million dollars felt relatively safe.

We passed the hotel gift shop, which was more like a small store. It had everything. I saw a pair of hiking boots in the window. Something about them called to me. I looked down at my well-worn dress shoes and thought I might need something a little more substantial for tonight's action. It was an impulse purchase. But, unlike the fedora I had bought in Miami the year before, it was one I wouldn't regret.

Stephanie was waiting at what was now our customary booth in the back. We joined her and Walton put the bags down on either side of him. One hand on each. He didn't want to let them out of his sight. Out of his touch. Even just for a moment.

A waitress came over, she was young and hip. I guess they scheduled the cool kids for Friday night. We all wanted a strong drink but ordered strong coffees. We would need all of our wits tonight, and then some. We would also need our strength. We ordered another round of burgers. Meat for Stephanie and me. Veggie for Walton. When the waitress left, we got down to business.

"Okay, Stephanie. What did you find out about Phil?"

"Bill, I'm sorry, but your friend is not who you think he is."

"Who is he then if he's not my friend?!" Walton pleaded.

As Stephanie broke it down for us, the big man fell silent. He listened as Stephanie explained that his old friend was the CEO of BioKerfin, a biopharmaceutical company of middling profits and little notoriety until fifteen years ago, when their tactics changed.

"They started buying up the product rights to drugs that treat specific diseases and increased the price. It started slow. They would just raise the price a few pennies, then a few dollars, then a few hundred dollars, then by a factor of fifty. With or without insurance, the medicine needed to save your life could cost as much as a new car. A new car you had to buy every month. Phil made a fortune while thousands of people died."

Walton sat back, soaking it in. Then something seemed to break inside the big man. His head dropped, as if his spine lost the strength to hold it up a second longer. He rubbed his face with his hands.

"Phil? Why?"

"I'm sorry, Bill. He did seem like a nice guy," I said.

"Thank you, Dave." Walton then reached over and palmed my head in his enormous hand. A gesture I would normally refuse, but in the current circumstances, silently accepted.

"So, Stephanie, who are these half a million suspects?" I asked, gently moving Bill's hand off my head.

"Well, I looked at the people who were most affected by the price increase. The people who died." She spoke with confidence, like she'd done this before. I realized, as a news producer, she had. Hundreds of times. "I eliminated everyone who didn't live in or around Seattle because, first off, there's no way I could look through half a million names in a few hours. And secondly, I had a hunch it was someone who lived in the area. So that narrowed the list down to thirty-three people."

She put a piece of paper down in front of us. A list of thirty-three names. Thirty-three people who died to make Phil Engels rich. Our coffee and burgers arrived. Suddenly I wasn't hungry anymore. Looking at Walton, I thought he might be sick right there at the table. We looked at the list of Phil Engels's victims. Josh Hogan. Kim Park. Marcus Anderson. And a name she had circled at the bottom of the page. I looked up.

"Enrique Bustamonte?"

Stephanie reached into her backpack and took out his obituary.

"Enrique Bustamonte lost his fight with acute myelogenous leukemia last Thursday evening at the age of forty-six. He is survived by his wife, Trudy Bustamonte, and his daughters Jackie... and Kaitlin."

Walton and I looked at each other.

"Kaitlin?"

Stephanie nodded. "I was looking for someone who lived in the area. I didn't expect them to be in her dorm room."

Chapter 27

Knock. Knock. Knock.

We were back in the UW dorms. This time with Stephanie. Grant, the same security guard from before, let us through in exchange for a Walton autograph while insisting that normally he would never do anything like this. I'm not sure Grant was a great security guard. Kaitlin Bustamonte opened the door wearing a flowy mustard-colored short sleeve dress and a rainbow headband.

"Oh. Hey. Did you find Abigail?"

"I think you know the answer to that question, Kaitlin," Walton said.

Kaitlin didn't blink. Unlike Ike, she had a pretty darn good poker face.

"I don't know what you're talking about. I'm actually pretty busy. I have a test to study for, so could you guys come back later?" She tried to shut the door but the frame bounced off the toe of Walton's size seventeen New Balances. Stephanie stepped in front of Walton, introduced herself, and pushed the door open. We entered the room, which was even messier now. It seemed like Kaitlin had started to occupy some of Abigail's space. Maybe because she knew she wasn't coming back? I shuddered.

"I'm sorry, but I already told you everything I know," Kaitlin said. "Abigail and I went to the Smokeshow together and I thought she bailed with some guy. Did you talk to Kern? She's probably tied up in his basement. He's a psycho."

Walton, maybe for the first time in his life, got right to the point.

"Kaitlin, we know."

"What do you know, Mr. Walton?" Again, she revealed absolutely nothing. I would not want to play poker with Kaitlin Bustamonte.

"Kaitlin. You are at a crossroads in your life," Walton said. "Like Bob Dylan at the Newport Folk Festival in 1965, but the path you are choosing is not leading to rock and roll immortality." Stephanie shot Walton a look that could freeze mercury.

"Kaitlin, I understand where you're coming from," Stephanie said. "You're over here with this old blanket and across the room Abigail's sleeping on Egyptian cotton. You've got a five-year-old Dell computer and she's got a brand-new MacBook Air." I looked around, impressed with Stephanie's powers of observation. I hadn't noticed any of this the last time we were in this room.

Stephanie's voice got quiet. Almost a whisper. "It's not easy being the poor kid at a rich school. Believe me. I know. I was also a scholarship kid at a big, fancy university."

"How'd you know I had a scholarship?"

"Because I lived in a dorm room just like this. With a filthy rich roommate who I hated. Only my roommate's father didn't kill my dad."

Kaitlin's poker face finally broke.

"We know what happened to your father," Stephanie said. "And we are so sorry."

Kaitlin sat down. She stared off into the middle distance. WIthout looking, she reached for an old quilted blanket and pulled it onto her lap.

"It wasn't my idea," she said, sniffling. "I didn't even want to do it."

Bill and I both stepped forward and Stephanie held up her hand, backing us off.

Kaitlin continued.

"Me and Abi were friends at first. For like the first week. We got along great. We did everything together. But then… We were at a mixer thrown by some stupid frat. We were talking about our families and she mentioned that her dad worked for a pharmaceutical company. I asked her which one and she told me. BioKerfin. I dropped my drink. Spilled everywhere. I felt sick. I played it off like I was wasted. I went to the bathroom and looked her dad up on my phone. He was the fucking CEO. I couldn't even look at her, so I bolted. I just got out of there. I went home and told my mom and my sister."

Stephanie didn't say a word. I sensed Bill and I should remain quiet as well. The less we talked, the more Kaitlin would.

"My sister freaked out. She wanted me to set Abigail's bed on fire with her in it. I just wanted to change roommates and be done with her forever. But my mom? She said I should just go back to school, keep being Abigail's roommate, and act like I didn't know. And that's just what I did. While my mom started to put together the plan."

"Wait. Your mom was behind this?" I couldn't stay silent any longer. When I imagined the kidnappers all this time, I certainly never pictured it being someone's mother.

"Yeah. It was her plan. She was in charge, as always. My sister and I did everything she told us to do."

"Where is Abigail?" Walton asked. "Where is she right now?"

"She's safe, Mr. Walton. We were never going to hurt her. We just wanted to make her father pay for what he did. Literally." She studied the floor.

"Okay, let's go." Walton led Kaitlin to the door.

"Are you taking me to the police?"

"Not yet." Walton said. "Right now, let's go get Abigail. She may not be kidnapped by crazed men who could kill her at any moment, but she doesn't know that."

"Will your boat fit all of us?" I asked.

"It's a twenty-five-foot Boston Whaler, there's plenty of— Wait. How'd you know we'd need a boat?"

Chapter 28

Kaitlin piloted the fishing boat through the calm waters of Lake Washington into a series of canals, called "cuts," which connected to Lake Union and finally to Puget Sound. The water got choppier after we passed through the Ballard Locks and into the Pacific. Kaitlin skillfully navigated around the many ferries, fishing vessels, and whale watching boats as the afternoon slid into evening.

Stephanie sat next to Kaitlin in the pilot house while Walton and I stood on the bow and looked west, towards the sunset. It was beautiful. A cracked pink glow at the end of the horizon encroached on all sides by darkness and gathering clouds. I shivered.

"I hate open water, Bill," I said, my voice cracking.

"I know you do, Pasch. Fortunately, it's a crystal clear night and the water is like glass!"

I looked up and saw clouds bubbling over the twinkling lights of the Seattle skyline. The wind picked up. If the water was glass, it was glass made by Chihuly. Twisting and spinning.

"I think that's a storm coming, Bill."

"All ahead full!" said Walton, enjoying himself a little too much. His voice had changed, become brighter. I chalked it up to the fact that we knew Abigail was in the hands of a mother and her daughter, not armed killers. It was a weight off our shoulders. The boat lurched and my stomach churned. Walton noticed me turning green.

"Dave! Feel the spray from mother ocean! Feel the blessings! Think of the creatures that lie within her depths. Orcas! Starfish! Dave! Aren't we lucky to be alive?"

"Yes. And I'd like to keep it that way." Words were a bit of a struggle now. It felt like I was swallowing a cup of saliva every second.

"Ship of fools, Dave. That's what we're on. A ship of fools!"

I couldn't take it anymore. I wandered into the pilot house with Stephanie and Kaitlin. Walton stayed at the front of the boat, arms extending up and over his head. Like a seven-foot hood ornament. Kaitlin noticed I wasn't feeling well and offered some advice.

"Focus on a specific point straight ahead. It'll help." I looked at the West Point Lighthouse. The place we were supposed to drop the money at one in the morning. I wondered where they would have left Abigail. I wondered a lot of things. I couldn't hold back my curiosity.

"Kaitlin, I have to ask. How did Ike get involved in all of this?"

"Well, when it was over, Abigail couldn't know we did it. She obviously knew me and had met my mom and my sister. We needed someone else to grab her for us. And a while back my sister dated a biker guy." She laughed. "A guy named Handsome Billy."

I chuckled. "I know Handsome Billy. He is very handsome."

Stephanie gave me a look.

"What? He is. I mean, he's not an ugly guy they call 'handsome' to be cruel. Like you'd call a fat guy Slim or a dumb guy Einstein." I stopped talking.

"Yes, Handsome Billy is good-looking, but he's a very bad dude. My sister hung around that crowd for years. She was in a real dark place back then. It was after my dad died. Drugs. In and out of jail. Anyway, she left him when she got clean. But when my mom said we needed someone to grab Abigail for us, Jackie knew who to call."

"But who were the other two men?"

"What other two men?"

"We know the bikers took Abigail and handed her off to two short, thick men with machine guns."

Kaitlin chuckled. "Two men who talked like this?"

She grabbed her phone and, after a few swipes and clicks, we heard the robot voice say, "Your money is in the bag, leave the girl and go."

"That was my mom and my sister wearing ski masks and padding under a few layers of clothes. Thanks to their outdated cis male gender role assumptions, the bikers saw two people with machine guns and assumed they were men. Just like you, Mr. Pasch."

I nodded, taking the hit.

She held up her phone. "We used this text-to-voice app whenever we had to communicate with anyone. You can make it sound like anything. Robot voice was the creepiest. When we did the exchange I was hiding with a Bluetooth speaker while my mom and sister kept their machine guns pointed at the bikers."

"If they had to, do you think they would have fired those guns?"

"We were praying it wouldn't come down to that, Mr. Pasch. Because they were fake guns. Well, they were air guns. If they pulled the trigger, Handsome Billy and his buddies would have gotten shot with a little BB. We bought them off Amazon and cut off the orange tips. Looked real, though. They certainly fooled Abigail," she said with regret.

"You were her roommate for the better part of a year," Stephanie said. "How did you pretend to be friends with someone you hated?"

Kaitlin considered the question for a moment.

"I didn't hate her. I still don't. I hate her dad. And, oddly enough, it was kinda easy to compartmentalize my feelings for Abigail and her father. Usually. I mean, sure, sometimes it was hard. When she showed up from a shopping spree with her mom. Or when some expensive new headphones showed up in the mail. I knew how they were paying for all that and it made me furious. So we didn't hang out all that much. Actually, that night we went to the Smokeshow was one of the first nights we had gone out together, just the two of us, since I found out about her dad." Kaitlin shook her head. "It's crazy but at one point that night I forgot what we were there for. I was just having a great time with her. I feel bad for Abigail. I do. None of this was her fault."

We heard Walton singing from the front of the boat. It was hard to hear, but I think it was a sea shanty he was making up. Kaitlin pointed to a small island just as we were passing it.

"We're here."

Then she turned, almost a full one-eighty, back towards a small cove, protected from the currents and completely hidden from view. If we weren't looking for it, we would have passed right by.

"My dad built a small cabin on this island years ago. We didn't own the land or anything, no one does. But he brought us up here all the time when we were kids whenever we needed a break from the city. It was just a tiny cabin with no electricity and no phones on a worthless pile of rocks, but it meant the world to him. He loved this place. And it was the perfect place to keep Abigail."

She worked the throttle and the wheel, slowing us down as we entered the cove. The boat, and my stomach, rocked as the water got even choppier.

"After we did the exchange, we had to send the video from the boat while we could still get a cell signal. Shooting that video was the hardest part. Watching her scream like that. She was terrified, of course. We needed her to be. But after that my mom gave her something to sleep. We carried her up to the cabin and I took the boat back by myself. That way, even if she escaped from my mom and my sister, she couldn't go anywhere."

Kaitlin turned to Stephanie. "Here, take the wheel. Head for the dock. When I give you the signal, cut the engines." I squinted and saw, poking out of the dark of the cove, a small wooden dock. Kaitlin ran to the front of the boat and stood next to Walton. After a moment she looked back and yelled.

"Now!" Stephanie cut the engine and the boat drifted to a perfect stop. Kaitlin pushed off the boat fenders and jumped onto the dock. Walton grabbed the line, flung it to her, and she tied it neat and fast around the cleat.

Kaitlin helped us all off the boat, took out a flashlight, and aimed it towards a dirt path leading to a wooden flight of stairs that zigzagged against the cliff looming over the cove. We climbed. Slowly and single file. The stairs were old but sturdy. They were well built.

The wind was starting to gale. I felt a few big drops fall, like scouts of an invading army. I almost lost my footing as a big gust seemed to come from the cove itself. I was thrown off balance and made matters worse with my unconscious reflex to grab at a handrail. But there was no handrail. I grabbed air and gravity, doing its dirty business, pulled me headfirst towards the rocks below. Just before taking a deadly tumble, a giant paw grabbed my shoulder and pushed me back onto the stairs. Walton. The big man's legendary reach came in handy once more.

Moments later we reached the top. I allowed myself to look down at the fifty-foot drop to the sea-sprayed jagged rocks below. I was grateful to be on solid land again. Even though it wasn't exactly solid. The meadow in front of us had turned to a marsh in the growing storm. I was thankful my new hiking boots were as waterproof as advertised. We headed towards a small cabin nestled at the edge of a dense forest. Light flickered from inside. Smoke curled up from a small chimney. Idyllic, if it wasn't hiding a kidnapped girl. We slowly, quietly approached the cabin.

"Okay," I whispered. "What's the plan? I mean, do we just knock on the door and say, 'Hello, we're here about the kidnapping?'"

Stephanie and I debated the best course of action. She thought we should send Kaitlin in first, to explain the situation and make sure there were no surprises.

And then Walton, being Walton, took a step back and knocked the door in with his shoulder. The door skidded open and he faced two women, one with grey hair, the other dark brown. They were identical, but for the generation that separated them. They were clearly Kaitlin's mother and sister. They sat at a small table, having dinner.

"Who the fuck are you?" Kaitlin's sister said. "You look like Bill fucking Walton!"

"Good," the big man said. "Because I am Bill fucking Walton." Somewhere, and I swear to God I wish it didn't happen, thunder clapped.

No one moved for a moment. Kaitlin's sister then jumped to her feet holding a very realistic-looking AK-47. Even though I knew it was fake, I flinched. I saw why it fooled Abigail and Ike. It looked very real to me. I prayed it hadn't been switched out for a real one.

"Jackie, stop. It's over." Kaitlin entered the cabin with Stephanie and me.

"Kaitlin, what are you doing here? This isn't part of the plan!"

"The plan's done, Mom. They know. They know everything." The two women sank, their shoulders dipping in unison. They seemed almost grateful it was over.

Kaitlin's mother unlocked the door and led us into a sparse but comfortable bedroom. It was far from the hell I had pictured Abigail spending the last three days. The windows were boarded up from the outside. On the queen-size bed, under the covers, was Abigail, sleeping peacefully.

"She's been like that most of the time," the old woman whispered. "We've been feeding her foods baked with heavy amounts of CBD oil. Figured it would keep her calm." Walton smiled.

"I've kidnapped myself that way a few times." I looked at him. "Highly recommend it. Incredible healing! This honestly might be very good for her nervous system. And it reduces inflammation."

I walked to her bed for a closer look. A battery-powered lantern on the nightstand gave a faint, warm light. Abigail was snoring lightly. A plate of fruit and cheese was on the bedside table, along with a bar of chocolate and a glass of water. She seemed fine. She even had her own bathroom. "Let's have a conversation," Walton said. "Do you have any coffee?" I asked.

"Sorry, no," Trudy apologized. "But I do have some kombucha. Hope you don't mind, it's high alcohol."

Walton smiled.

Chapter 29

We sat at the small table as Kaitlin poured six glasses from a pitcher of dark red liquid. "Delicious!" Walton said, sipping the kombucha. "Boysenberry?" Trudy nodded, impressed. Everyone sat and drank. Jackie tossed another log on the small wood-burning stove. The fire snapped and popped. Not wanting to be impolite, I took a small sip of the crimson potion. I was preparing for the worst and was pleasantly surprised. It was much better than Walton's bathtub concoction. I took a big swallow and I do believe I felt the enzymes doing their work. And moments later the high alcohol warmed me under my wet clothes.

"Mrs. Bustamonte—" Stephanie said.

"Trudy."

"Trudy. We know what happened to your husband and we're so sorry. But..." Stephanie paused, searching for the right words. "You seem like nice, normal people. How in the world did you do this?"

Trudy sipped her kombucha and then told us her story.

"My husband was a construction supervisor. And he was very good at it. He was doing so well he started his own company. As an independent contractor he was making more on his own than he had working for other people. Compared to most, we were wealthy. We had a nice home. We took vacations. Our daughters wanted for nothing. We had money saved up for their college educations. But then.... then he started getting tired. All the time. Which was strange for a man who had endless energy. He was losing weight. Then the nosebleeds. He finally went to the doctor when he woke up bleeding from his gums. We found out he had acute myelogenous leukemia. Of course, by the time we went to sleep that night I had become an expert in acute myelogenous leukemia. And I learned he would be fine. It was treatable and most often curable. I was so relieved. Then we found out the targeted therapy he needed would cost us thirty thousand dollars a month. Thirty thousand dollars! Even with our insurance, the copay was astronomical. Of course we paid. We had no choice. Enrique couldn't work, but I took another job. Then another. Then another. Jackie got a job to help pay. Even Kaitlin, as a ten-year-old, found ways to chip in. She organized fund-raisers at her school. She sold candy door to door. It just wasn't enough. The cost of the medicine drained us dry. And for Enrique, to be sick was one thing. To lie in bed and watch his family become destitute because of it… I think that destroyed him more than the disease."

I turned to Kaitlin and Jackie. Their heads were hung. They held each other. The story was hard to hear, I couldn't imagine what it must have been like to live it.

"Finally we were broke. We had nothing. We couldn't afford the next round of medicine. We were desperate. Jackie and I even… we robbed a bank."

"You did?!" Kaitlin was shocked; this was clearly the first time she had heard this. "Wait, I remember you coming home with all that cash that one time. You said that money was donated by a church!"

"The Church of Washington Trust Bank," Jackie smiled.

"A mother and her teenage daughter in ski masks with a note and radio parts taped to our stomachs. I think we were more scared than the people in the bank."

"And the money didn't even buy a month's worth of medicine," Jackie said with a grimace.

"I watched Enrique, my Kiki, fade before my eyes. The bank took our home. We had nowhere to go... But we still had the boat, he wouldn't let us sell that. So we brought him here. Finally being out of that bed, the sight of the island, the smell of it, invigorated him. He actually made it up those old deathtrap stairs on his own two feet. The last time he ever walked in his life."

She paused. No one said a word. No one breathed.

"We got him here. Put him in bed. He didn't have long and he knew it. But those last few days, he was at peace. Calm. He was so clear. He told us all how much he loved us. And how it was going to be okay. He died in my arms. His daughters by his side."

The sisters' heads were up now, watching their mother. They were crying. We all were. I turned to Walton and watched as clear, marble-sized tears rolled down his cheeks.

"We buried him here. In a special place..." Trudy shook her head, "Such a waste. A life just tossed away. I went to bed angry that night. And when I finally slept I had a dream. So vivid that it felt like something more... It was a vision. I saw a clinic. A place that would help people like my husband, like our family. Somewhere you could go when you couldn't afford lifesaving medication. A place that would take you in after the bank kicks you out of your home. And I knew who would pay for this place. BioKerfin. I decided to sue them for what they did to my husband. Our family."

Trudy laughed bitterly.

"Their lawyers were worse than leukemia. They destroyed me and my strip mall lawyer. They countersued. Those sons of bitches sued us. Us! I knew we could never win. Not that way. So I prayed. For ten years I prayed. And while I prayed, I worked. I took a job as a hospital administrator. I wanted to learn everything I could so I'd be prepared to run our clinic. Then, once my girls and I were finally back on our feet, I started to raise money. We had fund-raisers." She sneered. "Over ten years, do you know how much we raised? We raised five thousand dollars. It was a joke. Pathetic. Not nearly enough. We would need more. Much, much more. So I kept praying. Then one day Kaitlin ran home, telling us who her roommate's father was. The whole plan came to me in an instant. God had finally answered my prayers. God had shown me how we would pay for our clinic."

"Wait a second. Are you telling me God told you to kidnap Abigail Engels?" I asked, incredulously. "For her to be thrown in the back of a van by criminals? You do realize that this experience will affect her for the rest of her life?"

"Good!" Jackie spat at me. "Will Kaitlin and I not be affected for the rest of our lives by what her father did?! She should be affected!"

Trudy silenced her daughter with a look. Jackie instantly backed off. As much as Trudy seemed like a… for lack of a better term, an old kombucha-drinking hippie, she was clearly a force to be reckoned with.

"And what are the odds they'd be put together as roommates?" Trudy asked. "It boggles the mind. I couldn't help but see the divine in that. And we were never going to keep the money. Every cent was to go to the clinic we would build to honor my husband. Well, at least that was the plan." Trudy paused, taking a sip of her kombucha.

"But, over the past two days, I realized I've been a fool. Punishing Phil Engels wasn't God's plan. It was my plan. And I was wrong. This was wrong. I'll be praying again every night, Mr. Walton. This time for forgiveness."

The only sound in the cabin was the snapping of the fire in the stove. Then, without a word, Walton stood and left. I looked at Stephanie. Was he leaving? Was he bored? Calling the cops? What was he doing? Soon enough, as he returned, I realized he had gone back to the boat to grab the two fifty-five-pound bags of money. We had brought them with us because we certainly couldn't risk leaving ten million dollars in the back of my rental car. Walton walked back in and dropped the bags at Trudy's feet.

"This money is yours," Walton said. "You need it a hell of a lot more than Phil Engels does."

"You mean…"

"Open your clinic. We're not calling the police. Nobody goes to jail today. Justice has been done."

Trudy ran to Bill and hugged him around his waist. "Bless you, Bill Walton. You are the angel God sent to answer my prayers."

I wanted to clear my throat to indicate that maybe there was more than one angel doing the prayer answering, but Stephanie gave me a look that stopped me. Walton humbly accepted their thanks, then asked them to step out of the room while we got Abigail off the island and back to her family.

"We'll say we did the drop at the lighthouse and got her back safely from the mysterious kidnappers who vowed they would never return to harm Abigail ever again."

Trudy nodded solemnly. Walton turned to Kaitlin.

"Abigail will never know you had anything to do with it."

Kaitlin smiled sadly. There was no easy end to any of this. She'd have to go on pretending to be Abigail's friend. Pretending she had nothing to do with the kidnapping while helping her recover from the experience. The Bustamontes put on their coats and went out the back door of the cabin to a small covered porch. I closed the door and nodded to Walton, who went into the room where Abigail was still sleeping. He gently shook her awake. She woke up, blinking.

"Uncle Bill?" She was groggy. Then she realized where she was and what had happened to her. She bolted up, looking around for the armed men who took her. Walton calmed her down.

"You're safe now. Your parents paid the money. The bad men went away and they're never coming back. Now we're gonna get you out of here, Abigail. Okay?" She hugged Walton. He wrapped a blanket around her and brought her into the living room. Stephanie took a poncho she had stuffed in her backpack, put it on Abigail, and led her outside, carefully closing the door behind her. After they were gone, we brought the Bustamontes back in to say our goodbyes.

It was over. I took a deep breath and, for the first time in three days, I let my guard down. I think I laughed out loud, just enjoying the sheer relief of it all. Then I saw the door swinging open. I thought it was the wind. But it wasn't the wind. It was a man. A man holding a shotgun. It was... It couldn't be.

"Gibby?"

Chapter 30

"Shit! Bill Walton remembered my name! How 'bout that?!" Gibby walked into the cabin. It was like he was in slow motion. Walton and I locked eyes, our jaws agape. Utterly confused. But for some reason, deep down, I didn't panic. Even with a shotgun in his hands, I figured we'd be able to handle Gibby. Talk him out of whatever he was up to. After all, it was just Gibby.

Then I heard a voice that chilled my spine.

"Well, well, well, Bill Walton," Ike said, entering the room, smiling. "I've been to the fair and now I've seen the dancing bear." Ike brandished a Desert Eagle, a huge, powerful gun that looked like a toy in his giant hand. A gust of wind brought wet leaves scattering in behind him and, following the leaves, were Stephanie and Abigail. They were led back inside by Ike's cronies, Toucan and Handsome Billy, who wielded their own guns. Matching Heckler and Koch P-2000s with suppressors. Handsome Billy's megawatt smile faded when he entered the room and saw Kaitlin's sister.

"Jackie? What the hell are you doing here?"

"We're the ones who hired you to grab her, William."

"No, it was two robot dudes."

"That was us, you idiot."

"Well, well. Good to see you again, Jackie. Lookin' good." Ike leered at her and Trudy instinctively stepped in front of her daughter. "Thanks for the gig, but five grand feels like too small a slice of the ten million you got for her. So we've come for the whole fuckin' pie."

It occurred to me then that we were in fairly serious danger. In fact, we had entered into a situation that could be described as life threatening. I could hear Abigail's teeth chattering. She was shaking. She was scared. That was the proper reaction. Then she saw Kaitlin. She was confused at first, then she put it together.

"It was you?!" Abigail surged at Kaitlin but Toucan, who had a hold of her, didn't let go. Abigail thrashed and kicked but wasn't going anywhere past the huge, meaty arm restraining her. "Let me go! I'm going to kill you! I can't believe you fucking did this to me, you greedy bitch!"

"Fuck you!" Jackie shot back. "You think we give a shit about your money?! Our father died to get you that fucking money."

"What are you talking about?"

"Hey! Shut the fuck up! It's my money now. Where is it?" Ike found the bags without any help from us. He opened one and smiled a big, gold-toothed smile that didn't reach his eyes.

"What'd I say, Ike? I told you!" Gibby shouted. "Walton, I knew you'd lead me right to it."

"Gibby, you followed us?" Walton looked disappointed.

"I've been on your tail since you left my trailer. You didn't see me, did you?"

I thought back over the last two days and shook my head. I didn't notice anything. Gibby laughed.

"I knew it! Shit, nobody ever sees me. I've been invisible my whole damn life. It finally paid off. Once I saw you load the two big ass bags on the boat, I knew I found the money. I called Ike, told him everything, and he and the boys came a runnin'. We stole a speedboat and caught up to that big ass whaler y'all took off in. Shit, it was hard to miss."

Ike slapped Gibby on the back, knocking him forward a step. "Damn good work, Gibby. You're gonna earn your patch today."

"Hell yeah! Thanks, Ike! Hell yeah!" Gibby was giddy. Bouncing up and down.

"C'mon, Gibby. What about Speedwagon?" Walton pleaded.

"I guess you didn't listen to the lyrics, Big Red. You gotta roll with the changes."

"Gibby, I think you are completely misinterpreting the lyrics of REO Speedwagon," Walton said earnestly. Ike cracked his neck.

"You know what, Walton? You know what sucks? I'm gonna have to kill you before I get the chance to beat your ass. That's a damn shame."

"You're making a big mistake, Ike."

"How in the hell is killing you and pocketing ten million dollars a mistake?"

"Think of the karmic repercussions! The universe! Your very soul!"

Ike, Toucan, and Handsome Billy burst into laughter.

"Thank you for that, Walton," Ike chuckled. "Okay, let's go. Outside. All of you. We're tossing you off that cliff. Don't worry, it won't hurt. You'll be dead."

Ike motioned us outside with his gun. Gibby seemed confused.

"Hey, Ike?" Gibby said. "I thought we were just gonna like, take the money. We just want the money, right? You don't need to kill them. I mean, it's Bill Walton."

"Come on, Gibby. I'm not going to kill Bill Walton." Gibby exhaled, relieved.

"You are." Gibby's face turned pale.

"You want in, Gibby? You want your patch? You're gonna have to kill all these fuckers. Starting with him. You do that and I'll sew that bitch on myself."

I looked at Gibby and again saw the wheels slowly turning in his brain.

"But, it's just, you know, I really don't think we need to. We got the money, right? Can't we just leave them here? Tie 'em up or something?" Ike smiled.

"Gibby, don't worry about it. I was just playin'. But let me ask you one thing. How did you know about the ten million dollars?"

"Oh, that's easy. They told me about it, Ike. They came to my trailer asking about my van and I… uh…"

Ike finished his thought.

"And you told them I borrowed it. And you told them where to find me."

Gibby smiled a nervous smile. And then Ike shot him in the chest.

Screams filled the cabin as Gibby's body fell to the floor. Walton ran to help him but was held off by Toucan and Handsome Billy. Walton struggled like a lion surrounded by Roman soldiers holding spears. He roared. But it was done. Gibby was in a pool of blood that was slowly spreading over the cabin floor. Gibby was dead.

Trudy and Jackie tried to comfort Kaitlin, who was screaming hysterically. Stephanie tried to resist as Toucan shoved her and Abigail out the door and Ike, using his giant Desert Eagle as a conductor's baton, motioned for us to follow. We shuffled, zombie-like, as they led us out of the cabin, across the meadow in the pouring rain, to the edge of the cliff and its fifty-foot drop. I was stunned. To see a life snuffed out before your eyes is... Well, I couldn't dwell on it. Gibby's fate would soon be our own.

"Back 'em up! To the edge! After we shoot 'em, I don't want to have to work too hard pushing 'em over the cliff!" Toucan and Handsome Billy laughed as they forced us down on our knees with our backs facing the cove. Stephanie struggled, refusing to kneel.

"Don't do this," Stephanie said to Ike with a calm I couldn't have managed. "Killing us will sign your death warrant. Trust me, Ike. When they find my body they will know you did this—"

"Oh, they won't find your bodies." Ike took out his giant knife. "See, I'll cut your lungs out so you don't float. And, if you behave, I'll do it after you're dead." Handsome Billy kicked the back of Stephanie's knees, spilling her to the ground.

"William, please don't do this. You've got the money, please let us go," Jackie begged her ex-boyfriend.

"Sorry, babe. We had a good time, but not that good. Besides, after you got clean you got fat as shit." Ike and Toucan chuckled. They certainly seemed to be enjoying this.

"Okay. This is it. Any last words?" Ike asked. And that's when Walton started singing...

And this is where our story began. On our knees, on the edge of a cliff. It's cold, dark, and raining. Guns to our heads. Walton is singing a Grateful Dead song and I couldn't take it. Not another second. I could not die like this. I would not. That's when I turned to the men who were about to murder me and said...

"Please, for the love of God, kill Bill Walton first."

"What?" Ike and Walton said in unison.

"I beg of you. Kill him first. I need to see him die. Seeing him die will be worth my dying. Worth it a thousand times over."

"Pasch. My God..." Walton was hurt. "I thought you were my friend."

"I'm not your friend, Walton," I spat. "I've hated every moment of every day with you. Working with you is pure misery. Every single time you mention the Missoula Floods I've had to physically stop myself from strangling you with a microphone cord!"

"Dave, it's the geological event that shaped the American West—"

"Shut up! You've made my life a living hell! You've humiliated me on camera hundreds of times in front of millions of people! And now I'm going to die because of you. I'm here because of you. And I'll damned if you won't die first. So, please, Ike. Kill him! Kill this big, dumb son of a bitch right now or let me do it for you!"

Ike doubled over, laughing. Toucan turned his head to join in the mirth. They laughed harder, the way that two friends making eye contact while laughing somehow makes it funnier. Just a glance, a slight turn of his head. I saw Toucan's profile. And his giant Roman nose. Time was like molasses. I could see each raindrop landing in the thin light. Toucan's arm holding the gun aimed at me was pulled ever so slightly in the direction he was looking. Almost imperceptible. Just half an inch. Toucan hadn't noticed I had clawed the toe of my new Timberland boots onto a rock behind me. The traction was incredible. Like a starting block. He also hadn't noticed me coiling my entire body. Therefore he didn't react in time when I sprang forward, screaming with all the rage in the depths of my soul. Toucan turned and I saw his eyes go wide with… was it fear?

I focused on one thing. His nose. I was past the barrel when the gun went off. I was lucky. If the nine millimeter didn't have a silencer I would have lost hearing in that ear. I grabbed the arm that held the gun and used it to pull myself up, even faster towards my target. At the last second, I snapped my neck forward and down. My timing was perfect. I crushed his nasal cavity with the thickest part of my forehead. It made a crunch like a pit bull biting into a hard taco shell.

Ike turned to see what happened and Walton elbowed his forearm. The Desert Eagle flew to the ground. Ike backed up. He was fast and didn't let Walton hit him a second time. But he had to move at an awkward angle and was off balance. He stumbled over a rock and rolled away, into the dark.

Handsome Billy took a step back, confused. He was like one of those alien spacecraft that fell to the ground when they lost connection with their mother ship. Without Ike he couldn't function. This brief pause gave Stephanie all the space she needed. I saw the world-class athlete she once was combined with the combat training she had clearly picked up in a decade spent working in a war zone.

First, Stephanie disarmed him. I didn't see how. She was that fast. I did see the kick that sent Handsome Billy to his knees, which is when Stephanie really went to work. She was brutal. She unleashed a flurry of punches and kicks to his face that shattered those perfect cheekbones and snapped his chiseled jawline like a wishbone on Thanksgiving. I noticed Stephanie was a lefty and each punch she threw came with a little something extra. The diamond on her wedding ring sliced Handsome Billy's face to ribbons. After she was done with him, I'm pretty sure they just called him "Billy."

At the same time, the Bustamontes concentrated their attention on Toucan. I had broken his nose but the rest of him worked just fine. But not for long. Trudy, Jackie, and Kaitlin put him on the ground and kept him there with kicks to his head, body, and genitals from three different angles. I almost felt bad for him. Almost.

After the headbutt, I wasn't much help. I knew enough from covering football games that I should be in the concussion protocol. White spots danced before my eyes. My head throbbed. My skull felt like a church bell and my brain was the clapper. I felt my forehead; it was covered in blood. I didn't think it was mine. I looked around in a daze and there was Walton, smiling down at me.

"Nice work, Pasch! What a headbutt! Big Luke would have been proud!" He hugged me. "And what a speech. Ridiculous! I knew right away exactly what you were doing. Distraction! Tactics! How did you make up all those things about hating me? So many incredible details! Unbelievable!"

"Yes. Unbelievable, Bill. I just made it all up."

"I know you did! It was so absurd! It was art, Pasch. You're a genius. And you're a fighter, Dave. I knew you had it in you!"

I thanked him. It's funny. Walton's mantra had actually worked.

Preparation. Improvisation. Intimidation.

I had followed the Dancing Bears to the hotel gift shop and prepared myself with the impulse purchase of my hiking boots. If I had tried that move with my old dress shoes, my foot would have slipped right off that rock and we'd all be crab food right now. Then, I improvised that speech to distract Ike and, with a primal scream, by God I had actually intimidated Toucan. Buying myself the split second I needed to get my head past the barrel of his gun. Not too bad, Pasch, I told myself. Not too bad.

I smiled. Walton was dancing. You know, that Grateful Dead, twirly swim dance they all do. Whatever it was, the big man was happy and so was I. Stephanie brought us back down to earth. "Guys! Where's Abigail? And where's Ike?" We looked around. They were gone.

That's when the boat exploded.

Chapter 31

I turned to see the fireball rising from the Bustamontes' boat. It was in flames. And sinking.

"I guess Ike is down to one grenade," I said.

"Look!" Stephanie pointed. Illuminated by the inferno, I saw a speedboat cruising away from the island. I could see Ike holding Abigail and while I couldn't see the two bags of money, I could only assume Ike hadn't forgotten to take the ten million dollars with him.

Walton yelled, "Ike! Take the money! Just leave the girl!" But whether or not he heard him, the boat didn't change course and Ike didn't look back. Jackie Bustamonte came back from the cabin with some duct tape. She and Trudy bound Billy's and Toucan's hands and feet and taped their unconscious bodies to a couple of trees. We ran inside the cabin to get out of the rain.

"I think it's time to call the cops," I said as I took out my phone to dial. But I couldn't get a signal. "Anybody got any reception?" Bill and Stephanie took out their phones and shook their heads. The Bustamontes didn't bother checking. Kaitlin assured us they had never gotten a single bar of reception out here in the middle of Puget Sound. We were stranded. Well and truly. I sat down at the table to clear my thoughts. I checked my phone again. Habitually. Like opening the fridge when you already know what's in there. Nothing. Walton was getting more and more agitated.

"We've lost everything! Abigail. The money. Ike. What do we do?!"

"Relax," I found myself saying calmly. "How hard can it be to find a seven-foot-tall biker with ten million dollars? When the rain breaks, we'll flag down a boat and call the police. Ike will be locked up by morning."

"Canada." I heard a voice whisper.

"Who said that?" Walton's question hung in the air and was answered when we saw ripples in the pool of blood on the floor. Gibby was moving. Gibby was alive. Barely. Walton ran to his side.

"Gibby, stay with me. Hold on!"

"Canada." Gibby wheezed. He could barely whisper. "Ike… Ike's got a place… in Canada. That's where he's goin'…"

"Where, Gibby?! Where is Ike going?!"

"Don't know…" Gibby's breath was slow and shallow. "But I heard him… Said it's where… if things got… he'd… disappear… forever…"

Gibby's breathing slowed. Paused. Stopped.

"Roll with the changes, Gibby." Walton gently closed his eyelids.

"Okay, we need to stop Ike before he gets to Canada." I looked to Trudy. "How do we get off the island?"

"A ferry goes by every morning. I know the captain. If I signal, she comes by."

"That'll be way too late. There's got to be some other way," Stephanie said, pacing the room, looking for an answer.

"There is," Walton said as he stood, unzipped his fleece, and took off his shirt.

"We're swimming."

"Bill, it's miles to land. The water is forty degrees and there are eight-foot swells," I said. "You won't make it. Not in this weather."

"I've biked five hundred miles in a day. I can handle it but Pasch, you're gonna need a wetsuit. Someone get me the duct tape and as many garden trash bags as you can find."

"Bill, that's insane," Stephanie said firmly. "We're not swimming."

"Do you have a better idea?"

"No, Bill. I don't. But that's still an awful idea. I just wish we could—" Stephanie gasped, then silently cursed herself. "Oh my God, I am such an idiot." She ran to her backpack and pulled out what looked like one of those old Nokia cell phones, but it was red with a thicker antenna. "Satellite phone," she explained. "CNN gave me this when I was in Afghanistan. They never asked for it back and I just threw it in my bag in case I ever needed it. I'm sorry, I totally forgot about it. Is there anything in here that can charge it up?"

Jackie ran and got the battery-powered lantern from the bedroom. It had a USB port. Stephanie plugged in the phone and we all waited. It took a minute. A minute that felt like a year while five desperate people stared at a phone charging. Thankfully, this was one watched pot that boiled. The phone lit up and we cheered. Stephanie started dialing a number from memory.

"Put your shirt back on, Walton. I'm calling us a ride."

Chapter 32

Two hours later we were standing in a circle in the meadow between the cliff and the cabin. The rain had waned to a light spritz and, per Stephanie's instructions, we all had our cell phones out. Billy and Toucan had regained consciousness and were none too happy about being taped to trees in the rain with busted faces. Over the past few minutes their threats had evolved into some sincere, rather pathetic begging. None of us cared.

"If we swam, we could have been halfway there by now," Walton complained.

"Bill, what's the capstone on top of the Pyramid of Success?" Stephanie asked, like a teacher talking to a petulant student.

"The capstone is split into two philosophical building blocks for winning at basketball and life," Walton said, then smiled as he understood. "Faith. And patience."

"Bingo," Stephanie replied. Then, in the distance, I heard a rumble. It could have been thunder but it seemed to get louder. And closer. And it got closer in a hurry. Whatever the thunder was, it was moving fast.

"Okay," Stephanie cried. "Now!"

We lifted our cell phones, which despite their lack of signal, were not completely useless. They still had working flashlights. We pointed them in the air. Lighting up our little circle. The thunder turned into a roar. Then we saw it. A Black Hawk helicopter shot up from the cove and hovered over our improvised landing zone. It made a ninety degree turn and slowly lowered itself down. It paused fifteen feet off the ground and two black ropes flew out of either side of the chopper.

Two men in full combat gear zipped down the lines. They landed and quickly, efficiently swept the vicinity, each with a semiautomatic rifle raised to their cheek. Seconds later they gave a signal and the chopper dropped the final fifteen feet, runners sinking into the wet ground. The pilot cut the engines and the roar of the blades turned into a whisper.

A half-dozen more soldiers spilled out of the Black Hawk, making a perimeter around the man who came out last. A tall, ruggedly handsome Hispanic man who moved with the easy grace and confidence of a professional athlete. According to the patches and insignia on his uniform, this was Colonel Cabrera of the United States Army. I went to thank him but he walked by me and kissed Stephanie right on the lips. I guess they knew each other?

Stephanie broke off the kiss and turned to us. "Bill, Dave. I'd like you to meet my secret government source, and my husband, Elvin. Who, luckily for us, is currently stationed down in Medford, Oregon."

So, this was the guy Stephanie met in the Middle East and decided to start a family with.

"Nice to meet you, Mr. Walton. Big fan," the Colonel said.

"And this is Dave Pasch." Stephanie pointed to me. The Colonel gave me a firm handshake, but not one of those knuckle-crushers made by insecure guys who treat every handshake like a test of their masculinity. The Colonel's handshake seemed to say, "I could easily kill you, but let's be friends."

"Oh, Dave Pasch needs no introduction," the Colonel said. "I'm a big fan of yours as well, Dave. I don't know how you keep it together with this guy sometimes." He nodded to Walton. "I'd love to get your autograph." I smiled. I liked this guy.

"Wait," Stephanie said to her husband. "Where's Ana?"

"Don't worry, our daughter is in good hands. I left her with the Commander in Chief." The Colonel winked at us. "My mom." Then he got down to business. "Okay, Stephanie gave me the sitrep and we are a go to assist with your situation. For the sake of plausible deniability, I don't want to ask too many questions. Let's just say we are running a training exercise. So, where is this training exercise headed to next?"

Walton smiled. "Colonel, I just want to take a moment to say that I was with you and every one of your military brothers and sisters throughout the entire Vietnam experience. I realize it was the civilian leadership, not the—"

I cut Bill off, knowing full well how much time this detour could cost us.

"We're headed north, sir!" It just felt right to call him "sir." "To the Canadian border. We need to find a big man headed to Canada with—"

"Let's just leave it at that," interrupted the Colonel. "Again, the less I know the better." He turned to his team. "Thirty seconds and this bird is in the air!" They snapped into action. A soldier approached.

"Colonel! What do we do with the two, uh…" He nodded over at Toucan and Billy. The Colonel laughed. "Soldier, it appears two men have duct-taped themselves to a couple trees of their own volition." He walked over to Toucan and Billy, who were thrown into a terrified silence by the unexpected arrival of the U.S. Army. The Colonel inspected the right side of Billy's face and turned to Stephanie. "I see this guy has met my wife's left hand." She held up her bloody wedding ring and apologized. "Don't apologize, honey. That's exactly why I picked out that ring. It was always supposed to be a symbol of our love and a weapon of self-defense. Are we taking them with us?"

She nodded.

"Okay, we'll take them back to the base and our MPs will make sure they find their way to the nearest police station."

"Thanks, Colonel. I owe you one," Walton said.

"No, Walton. You owe my wife one," the Colonel corrected. "And welcome to the club."

Toucan and Billy were unceremoniously dumped into the helicopter and, as I turned to jump on board myself, I noticed the Bustamontes were not moving. I waved them towards us, but Trudy shook her head and looked to the cabin. Bill and I walked over to her.

"We can't just leave him in there like that. We'll clean him up and, in the morning, we'll flag down the ferry and take him to the authorities."

"But, if you go to the cops you'll have to explain what happened."

"A man has died," Trudy said firmly. "This is over. No more hiding. No more secrets. We go to the police and what happens, happens."

Jackie and Kaitlin stood behind their mother. In every way possible.

"Bill! Dave! We gotta go!" Stephanie yelled behind us.

We nodded. Bill wrapped the three women in one giant hug and said something I missed under the growing roar of the helicopter. Whatever it was, it made Trudy laugh. Then she wiped the tears that came pouring out of her eyes. I never asked Bill what he said to her. It was their moment.

I waved goodbye and we ran to the chopper. I made sure Bill bent down, clear of the blades. He stepped right into the chopper while I was pulled up and into it by Stephanie and one of the soldiers. The Black Hawk lifted up off the ground. The Bustamontes waved to us and got smaller and smaller as we went up over the tree line. Then we saw the entire island. The Bustamontes' special, hidden place. The place they came to escape the city. The place where two men had died. Died for money. Stupid money. The Black Hawk turned east and the island disappeared in the mist behind us.

Chapter 33

I held on for dear life as the helicopter sped back towards land. I was in the belly of a roaring beast. A very different experience from the helicopter tour my wife and I had taken into the Grand Canyon years ago. We weren't doing any sightseeing tonight. The ocean was a dark, undulating blur beneath us. One of the soldiers gave Walton, Stephanie, and me helmets. They had microphones and earpieces that reminded me of the headsets we wear during games and we were finally able to talk over the sound of the chopper. We agreed it was unlikely, if not impossible, Ike would take the speedboat all the way to Canada.

After some "gentle prodding" from the Colonel, Toucan and Billy gave us a description of Ike's motorcycle. "A Chief with ape hangers." We looked at them blankly until Toucan explained, "It's a giant fucking hog with big ass handlebars." Moments later we were rocketing up the coast, parallel with I-5. We saw plenty of vehicles and a few motorcycles but no "ape hangers." No Ike. No Abigail.

We got as close to the Canadian border as we could and turned back. I did the math and there was no way Ike could have already crossed the border. Not on a bike. The Colonel's voice sounded in our headsets, "He must be on one of the old roads. Before the I-5 was built, there were a few old two-lane highways that carved through the mountains, up to Canada."

"You from this area?" Walton asked.

"Close enough. I was born and raised in Portland," the Colonel answered. Then he raised his shirtsleeve to reveal a tattoo of a red and black pinwheel Bill Walton knew very well. It was the logo of the Portland Trail Blazers. "Like I said, I'm a big fan."

Walton put his hand over his heart and nodded.

We spent five or ten desperate minutes searching the small "old roads" that wound through the northernmost reaches of the continental United States. And, on one such road, just five miles from the Canadian border, we found them. A single motorcycle with two riders. Someone handed me binoculars. They were good. Very good. I could see everything clearly, down to the giant red eyeball tattoo on the back of a hand gripping one of the "ape hangers." It was Ike all right. Abigail was behind him, her hands secured to the bike with zip ties. Two leather duffles stuck out of the saddlebags. Ike maintained his speed. He had no way of knowing the military bird flying far over his head was chasing him. We passed ahead of him about a mile and heard the Colonel's voice on the headset.

"Okay, I called it in. During our 'training exercise' we happened to notice what looked like a girl in trouble on the highway. Canadians have agreed to stop border traffic and local police are heading up from Ferndale."

"He's trapped!" I said, excited.

"I don't know," Stephanie said. "The Canadian border is four thousand miles wide. You're telling me they're going to shut down every single little road and dirt path in and out of there? If there's a secret way to get through, I bet Ike knows it."

The Colonel's brain immediately clicked to the next solution.

"Okay, option two. We set this bird down in front of him and use the full power of the U.S. Army to stop that man from reaching the border."

"No good." Walton shook his head. "Colonel, if we land in front of Ike and point a dozen guns at him, either of two things will happen. One, he'll kill Abigail. And I can't let that happen. Or, more likely, he'll call our bluff. He knows we can't do anything while he's got her and he'll ride right past us and disappear into Canada with Abigail and ten million dollars. I can't let that happen either."

It was quiet then. Well, as quiet as it could be in a Black Hawk helicopter hovering a hundred feet off the ground.

"Option three," Walton said. "Set this bird down, drop me off, and get out of here."

"What the hell are you talking about?"

"There's only one thing Ike wants more than ten million dollars. He wants to kick my ass."

I looked at him, incredulously.

"To save Abigail, you're willing to let Ike beat you up?"

Walton smiled. "I didn't say that. I said he wants to kick my ass. He'll stop to fight me. I didn't say he'd win."

"Come on, Bill. You don't stand a chance. He's got three inches on you, a hundred and fifty pounds, and he's thirty years younger."

"Stephanie, what have I told about putting numbers in my ears?"

I couldn't help but smile along with Stephanie. The pilot's voice interrupted our conversation.

"Colonel! Fuel's in the black. If we don't leave now, we're walking home. What's my order, sir?" The Colonel looked to his wife for his orders. She nodded.

"Set it down, Lieutenant! We're dropping one off and heading home!"

"Dropping two," I shouted in my microphone. "I'm coming with you, Bill!"

"Pasch, please!" Walton scoffed. "Why?"

"Because we're partners, Bill! When are you going to get that through your giant, thick head?" Walton smiled.

"Okay, we're dropping off two!"

"Three!" Stephanie shouted. "We're a team. We do this together."

We landed on the only available space between the endless miles of fir trees. Right on the highway. We hopped out of the Black Hawk as the Colonel yelled after us. "We'll tell the local police to look for you as they come up!" The Colonel looked to Stephanie. "Be careful!"

The Colonel gave the signal and Black Hawk took off, leaving us on the highway. Moments later, the deafening roar of the helicopter had been replaced with the silence of a predawn forest. After a few seconds my ears starting working again. I could begin to hear the proverbial early birds, chirping in the trees around us. I could hear the wind gently pushing the leaves around. And then, in the distance, a far less welcoming sound. The low, rumbling engine of a motorcycle.

Chapter 34

It was morning, but just, and the highway was still dark. The storm that soaked the land the night before was long gone. To my right, the forest continued to sleep in darkness. To my left, the clouds had big gaps between them and through that, strong blue light crept up the evergreens. The old road was no simple highway. It was the line between the light of dawn and the dark of night. We looked ahead to the sharp bend in the road, where Ike would soon appear.

"What's the plan, Bill?" Stephanie asked.

"Follow the Dancing Bears."

"Not sure I understand that."

"Don't worry," I said. "I do."

Walton smirked, then turned back to the road. "You two need to stay clear. No matter what happens, don't jump in. This fight needs to be just him and me."

"You got it," I said.

"Bill, there's no way I'm going near him. This is all you, big guy," Stephanie said, patting him on the back. Walton looked like he had expected us to offer a little more resistance, but nodded. Stephanie and I darted off the highway and easily disappeared into the trees.

Walton stood on the broken yellow line in the middle of the road when Ike finally turned the corner. He slowed down and stopped about ninety-four feet from Walton. I swear to God, it was the length of a basketball court. Ike got off the bike and I saw Abigail, eyes closed, her hands behind her back. Ike pulled out his Desert Eagle. He lifted the gun in the air and made a show of putting it down on the seat of his bike. I guess Walton was right. Ike really did want to kick his ass.

The two giants walked towards each other in the middle of the two-lane highway like monsters in a Japanese movie. I felt like an extra in one of those movies. A tiny, trembling citizen of Tokyo watching two titans on a collision course. With no telling what sort of collateral destruction they would cause. And no power to stop it.

They waited until they got close. Arms down. Unblinking.

"You're in my way, hippie."

"Friend, you've got something that doesn't belong to you. Give it back. You can keep the money, Ike. Just leave the girl and enjoy your trip to Neil Young's homeland."

"Nah. I'm gonna hold on to both for a little while, just in case there are any more surprises up the road. I just need to put you down first. I told you, Walton. If I saw you again I'd beat your ass."

Ike reached in his T-shirt. He pulled out a necklace with a small horn attached at the end. Like a miniature version of what Civil War soldiers used to carry gun powder. He unscrewed the horn. He tapped out a pile of beige powder on the back of his hand and put it to his nose, snorting a golf ball-sized bump into both nostrils.

Ike offered Walton the powder horn.

"Care for a little getgo powder?"

"Speed kills, Ike. Stick to plants."

"Oh, this ain't speed, hippie. It's meth. I'm gonna enjoy this."

They inched closer. Now inside the range of each other's enormous reach. Arms still at their sides. A blinking contest. A duel of intimidation. Godzilla and King Kong playing chicken. Who would give in? Who would cave?

The first punch was Ike's.

He drew his power from the ground. His feet were well planted and his knees were bent. He came from a crouched position, building his momentum from his legs to his shoulder. Then exploding forth, twisting his arm in a hook bound for Walton's chin.

It didn't miss.

Walton was spun by the knock. But he still was able to sense that the first punch was just one piece of the two piece Ike was cooking up. The curling left was aimed at his head. It was meant to be a finishing blow but Walton, reeling as he was, still had his footwork. He cut down on the angle. Ike's punch carved through the air but overreached.

He missed.

He was exposed.

Walton turned, cutting the target for Ike to hit in half. Boxing was a bloodsport of angles. The angle you offered had to be to your advantage and your opponent's disadvantage. I'm not sure Walton knew anything about boxing, but he was a master of angles. And he had the advantage now.

But Walton couldn't throw a punch the way Ike did. His legs, where all the power of punches comes from, wouldn't allow it. Walton's legs were a constant source of agonizing pain for him. I can't imagine the suffering of having a foot split in two lengthwise. A foot that broke again and again in the four seasons Walton missed in the middle of what should have been his prime. I can't imagine the agony of thirty-seven orthopedic surgeries up and down both legs. Walton wasn't using his legs, because he couldn't use them. He had to find another way.

So Walton's power came from his upper body. He generated torque from the twist of his hips. It had to be timed perfectly. He swayed left, then right. Like a python. Got his rhythm. He gathered everything he had. Then he struck. His long arm and enormous hand had their own momentum, like a rocket ship breaking out of the atmosphere and into the vacuum of space.

Ike missed blocking the punch by a quarter of an inch. Unfortunately for him, a quarter of an inch was all Walton needed. He landed the blow to Ike's left cheek. Splitting the skin. Ike fell back, out of Walton's range. He took a beat to recover, then charged.

Now it was Walton's turn to be on his heels.

Ike roared. A kodiak bear in a leather jacket. Walton did all he could with his angles. Used his arms as protection. It didn't matter. Ike unleashed a double right hook to the body. The first one opened him up. A pathfinder. The second one connected. Bang. Walton was rocked. A stunningly painful blow. He staggered. Somehow staying on his feet. Ike tried a straight jab.

This time, Walton was ready.

He twisted, again gathering power like a spring. He dodged the jab and threw his own. It landed and Ike pirouetted involuntarily. It was almost graceful.

The big men stood there. Panting. Bleeding. They had traded punches. For average men, these would have been mortal blows. But these were far from average men.

"Why you doing this, Walton? You ain't gonna change anything. You're just slowing me down and pissing me off." He spat. Phlegm and blood.

"If you plant ice you're gonna harvest wind," Walton said. "You've planted your ice. Now consider me the wind."

Ike whirled, arms extended, a spinning elbow. It was an MMA move. Vicious. But it looked like a basketball move. Like a post player extending his elbow to make space for his spin move. Ike's arm increased speed and headed for Walton's face. But Walton's footwork was too good. Too practiced. His muscle memory stretched back decades. He didn't think.

Walton pulled the chair.

After leading him to believe he was matching his body weight, Walton took a step back as Ike's elbow started to swing. Ike spun too fast and his own momentum, expecting contact with Walton, found nothing. Nothing but pavement. Ike hit the ground. He quickly rolled over and got up on one knee. That's when Walton hit him with a good old fashioned right cross that turned Ike's head like an owl's. Ike fell to the ground and hit his head on the pavement. Ike was down. He was stunned. Hell, so was I.

"You hear that?" Stephanie nudged me. It didn't seem like she had even been paying attention to the fight. She was looking south. Towards the very faint but approaching sound of police sirens. "If they show up and pull a bunch of guns, this is all over and Abigail dies. Probably along with Walton."

"Okay. One of us needs to run down the road and hold the cops off and the other needs to cut Abigail loose from that bike." I paused. "I guess I'll run down the road and stop the cops?"

Stephanie gave me a withering look.

"What? I know you hurt your knee back in college."

"Pasch, I could outrun you with two bad knees. As long as I don't need to make any cuts, I'm fine."

She reached into her backpack and handed me a pocketknife.

"Cut Abigail loose. And make sure Ike doesn't see you."

"What else you got in that backpack?"

Stephanie smiled and then, after checking to be sure Ike wasn't looking, started to run. Slowly at first and with a slight limp. Then almost skipping. Then full out running. Sprinting. A hundred yards, maybe more, then she disappeared around the bend in the road. I looked to Ike, who was still on the ground, stunned. He hadn't noticed Stephanie or the sirens. Good. I started moving through the trees, towards Abigail, keeping my eyes on Walton and Ike.

Walton was winded. He held himself up by pushing on his knees. Ike got up. Slow. He lost round one. Bad. But his confidence was not shaken.

"Shit. That all you got, hippie?"

"That's not all I got," Walton said. "But that's all you want."

Walton's advantage was short-lived because it appeared the meth Ike snorted had just kicked in. His eyes went wide as the chemicals reached his central nervous system. It fired him right up. He howled into the air like a wolf on a blood moon. Then, a blur of leather. Ike stormed at Walton, throwing punches. A jab directed at Walton's nose. Walton dodged. The wrong way. Ike connected. Pushed Walton's nose back. Ike wasn't done. A right hook to the ribs exploded Walton's guard. He was wide open for the third. A meaty right cross that detonated like a missile. Walton's neck twisted back. Blood gushed from his nose. Walton had taken three heavy shots. I didn't know if he could take a fourth.

This round the scorecard was solidly in Ike's favor. And Ike pushed the upper hand. He was spam punching now. Unleashing a fury of combinations. Everything must have told Walton to back away but Walton didn't back away. Walton stepped closer. Smart. By decreasing the length Ike had to punch, he was reducing the power of the blows.

But this tactic cost Walton dearly.

He was getting pummeled. Mauled. Ike was peppering shots all over his body. Kidneys, liver, chest, face. He was picking his spots. Walton's long arms did his best to block the force of most of them but they kept coming. Jab, jab, hook. Jab, jab, cross. Then two more body shots to Walton's left side. Walton blocked those with a desperate stab. He didn't sidestep the next barrage. Absorbing Ike's onslaught.

Ike kept throwing punches.

Walton kept taking them.

They were so close they looked like they were slow dancing. Toe to toe. Ike was breathing hard now. Sweating. Bill was bleeding. Badly.

"Look at you, Walton! You haven't even touched me! I'm gonna fucking murder you."

Walton laughed.

Wait, he laughed?

Yes, by God, he was laughing.

"You think you're causing me pain, Ike? I've battled Artis Gilmore, Bill Laimbeer, Kareem Abdul-Jabbar! This is a pillow fight. You're tickling me."

Ike growled and drove his shoulder into Walton's chest, pushing him back. It gave him the space he needed to fire an uppercut. Bam! Walton took the punch, smiling. Ike laid a few more jabs from his toes. Punching down at Walton.

"Does it hurt yet, hippie? Does it?!"

More punches. Thunderous punches that seemed to come from the tops of the trees to land on Walton's face. Walton couldn't keep being a pacifist. He needed to start fighting. But he didn't start fighting. He started talking.

"You think you understand pain, Ike?" Walton wiped blood from his mouth. "You don't understand anything." Ike tossed a speculative hook that Walton could have easily blocked but he allowed it to connect. Walton was letting Ike hit him.

"Pain has been my companion my entire adult life. I live with pain. I learned to love pain. Through pain I have been reborn." Without warning, Walton sent a karate chop that struck Ike's throat. Catching him in the Adam's apple. Ike recoiled.

"Feel that? That's my good friend, Pain. He wants to come over to Ike's house to play," Walton said. Ike gasped and growled, trying to catch his breath. "You think you know me? You don't. If you did, then you wouldn't have underestimated me. I should be dead. I broke my foot in half, I kept playing the game. My spine collapsed, I kept living my life. I've had my flesh opened and my bones fused together. You think you can hurt me? You think I'm afraid of you? Who are you to defeat me?!"

Ike attacked. Hit Walton with a left. A right. Again. And again. Walton just let Ike swing and hit. He took the shots. Hard ones. Walton showed no effect other than more cuts opening up under his eye. It was starting to freak Ike out.

"You tired, Ike?" Walton asked.

"You've just begun to bleed," Ike said, breathing hard. His heart not quite in it anymore.

Then Walton ended the fight. It was like he took the energy of every punch Ike had landed on him and channeled it into his right arm. He took his fist, made a bomb, and threw that bomb into Ike's kidney.

It was Krakatoa. Vesuvius. Primordial. The punch was cosmic.

The sound of it landing was like a jet breaking the sound barrier. Upon its impact a flock of birds fled the trees. I was hit with a shock wave, like a house at a nuclear test site. I was literally knocked backwards.

Ike gasped, breathless. A proper kidney shot will suck the air out of your body like opening a space lock on the ISS. This particular kidney shot was an extinction level event. It completely obliterated the normal function of his internal organs. Ike was well beyond winded. He fell straight to the ground, like a marionette whose strings had been cut.

I ran to Abigail.

"Holy shit, did you see that?" she asked me. "I think he just killed the bastard."

"How are you?" I asked as I cut through the zip ties that bound her to the bike.

"I'm fucking exhausted. How am I this tired?"

"You've been sedated with heavy amounts of CBD oil. Don't worry, it's safe. It's just making you very tired. And apparently reducing your inflammation. Come on, we have to get out of here." I led her back into the woods, keeping my eyes on Ike, which is why I didn't see Abigail grab the gun off the seat of the motorcycle.

Ike was flopping like a fish in a bucket but he managed to reach into his jacket and pull out his giant blade. Having the knife seemed to give him energy. Impossibly, Ike got back to his feet. Walton shook his head.

"C'mon, Ike. I thought this was a fistfight," Walton said. "Now you're bringing cutlery to the table? Bad manners."

"We're out of time, Walton. I gotta gut you and get gone."

Walton moved backwards to miss Ike's wild swings of the blade. Ike's range was limited as he had to keep one arm pinned to his gut, where Walton's blow still reverberated. But he was on the offensive. He moved forward, crouching, chopping, slicing. A madman with a ten-inch knife. Walton was playing defense. Backing up. Moving his feet. Ike tried to grab and stab. Walton wrenched free. Stepped back in retreat. Ike advanced. Then Walton stopped retreating and moved in. He blocked Ike's arm holding the knife and slammed an elbow to the side of Ike's head. Ike barely felt it. Must be the "redneck cocaine" he had surging through his veins. Ike put both hands on the knife, lifted it above his head, and stabbed down at Walton's neck with all his might.

It took both of Bill's hands to block it at the wrist but Ike kept pressing. He was betting that he was stronger than Walton. It seemed a good bet. He was slowly pushing the knife towards Walton's windpipe. Walton's arms were pushing him away, but giving, his muscles spasmed. Their bodies shook with effort. Their arms vibrating. It was like watching a deadly arm wrestling competition. And Walton was about to lose.

The knife got closer. Closer. Ike now had his full body weight on the hilt of the knife. Walton struggled to get away. But he couldn't. The tip of the blade cut into Walton's neck. Just a millimeter or so but blood started leaking out of the tiny wound. Encouraged, Ike pushed down harder. Harder. Walton couldn't hold out a second longer. He also couldn't take his hands off the knife that was about to decapitate him. There was only one thing he could do. It would be unthinkably painful, but he had to do it. He had to use his legs.

Ike was on his right side, so Walton stepped back with his left foot. His devastated, broken, mangled left foot. He brought it back about six feet and then kicked it as hard as he possibly could into Ike's knee. I'm not sure who screamed louder, Ike or Walton. The kick was torture for Walton, but it worked. Ike's knee bent back in a way a knee shouldn't. He hit the ground. Hard. Knife skittering across the highway.

Walton was still standing. Somehow.

If there was a referee they would have counted to about eight or nine. Then incredibly, Ike pushed himself up to stand on his last good leg. And then the bad news, Ike took the last grenade that swung from his belt and pulled the pin.

"Hold it right there, asshole!"

It was Abigail. She stepped forward, pointing the Desert Eagle at Ike. Bill had his back to us and he turned to see what was happening.

"Abigail, no. Put the gun away," Walton pleaded.

"I'm not going to let him kill you."

Ike laughed.

"I'm not gonna kill him. I'm gonna kill you and let him live the rest of his long, hippie life knowing he got you, and that little bald guy, all blow'd up."

Ike took aim. He positioned the grenade to throw. Dropped it deep behind him. Ready to lob it high. Like a hook shot. Right at us. We froze. We didn't move. We couldn't move.

Walton moved.

It is said the sky hook is the only truly unguardable shot in basketball. A truism that usually holds but for one important factor: the person shooting it has to have the proper fundamental technique. Tim Duncan comes to mind. Shaquille O'Neal, known for his power, had an underrated baby hook. Bill Russell won eleven championships with his left-handed hook. Walton's wasn't too shabby. Wilt. Yao. Hakeem had a few great hooks mixed into his legendary Dream Shake. And, of course, there was the master: Kareem Abdul-Jabbar. Thanks in part to the NCAA banning the dunk during his collegiate career, Kareem perfected the fundamentals of the sky hook.

Ike had not.

He didn't put up his forearm, like Jabbar would have done. Ike was used to executing this shot against lesser, shorter opponents. He wouldn't have lasted a season in the NBA. Walton lasted thirteen.

Walton took a step forward and blocked it right out of Ike's hand.

Swat.

The grenade carved back through the air. A perfect arc. Into the trees where the stands would have been. It exploded, sending bark and rock in every direction. Abigail and I hit the ground. We were fine. Dirty, but fine.

Ike staggered. Holding his side. He slumped to his knees. He was bleeding. He'd been hit. Large splinters of shrapnel stuck in his gut and side. Walton was okay. Ike was taller and wider than he was and standing right in front of him. He took the full force of the blast. Ike fell to the ground, beat. He had no more dirty tricks up his long leather sleeve.

My phone rang. It was Stephanie.

"Are you okay?!"

I explained what happened and gave her the green light to send the cavalry.

Walton walked over to Ike.

"Not bad, Walton," Ike said. "Not bad. No one ever blocked it like that."

Walton knelt down beside Ike as the sirens approached. When the police took Ike into custody, Walton was still teaching him the fundamentals of the sky hook. I looked at my watch and did the math. With police escort we'd make it back to Seattle just in time for the tournament final. We had a game to call.

Six months later...

Epilogue

The skies were clear and blue and the leaves of the trees shimmered in late summer splendor. Specks of yellow punctuated the serrated leaves of the aspens sprinkled throughout the evergreens. Occasional high clouds floated by, but visibility was clear. We could see the peaks of Mount Rainier. Mount Olympia. Even Mount St. Helens with its signature flat top.

Mount St. Helens. Blown apart in 1980. Forever changed. But not dead. Still there. Forever. The volcano was an epic reminder of life's bigness and its danger. Scientists were shocked when the forests, completely destroyed by the eruption, grew back much faster than they expected. The ash acted as fertilizer. Walton stood still as a mountain. I stood next to him. We both watched and listened.

"The Enrique Bustamonte Memorial Clinic will be a place of hope for those lost in the cracks of America's broken health care system," Trudy Bustamonte said proudly to the crowd of people and reporters standing before her. Her voice echoed, amplified by the PA. She was surrounded by orange balloons. Orange, the color of awareness for the disease that killed her husband.

"This clinic has been a dream, a vision of mine for a long time. I tried everything I could to get it going. And thanks to…" She smiled at Phil and Helen Engels, who looked very different from the time I last saw them. Happy. Peaceful. "Thanks to an anonymous ten million dollar donation, I was finally able to build my dream."

When Abigail learned what her father had done to Kaitlin and her family, and to thousands of other families, she refused to say she had been kidnapped. Abigail insisted the whole thing was her idea and demanded Phil and Helen drop all charges against the Bustamontes. Ike was convicted of Gibby's murder. Bill still writes to him in prison, urging him to change his ways. Ike is playing basketball again, apparently dominating the Federal Detention Center in SeaTac with an unstoppable sky hook. Good for him.

"And we are proud to open the very first open-source medication clinic in the country. The first of many! These clinics will be a beacon of hope where people who need lifesaving medicine are able to receive it. A place of healing. A place of redemption."

The crowd applauded enthusiastically. The clinic was beautiful. A stunning, glass structure in a pristine location a half-mile from the east edge of Lake Washington. It sparkled in the sun. Trudy Bustamonte grabbed the giant novelty-size scissors and proudly cut the orange ribbon in front of its doors.

"It's beautiful. Isn't it, Walton?" I asked.

"It's glorious. A monument to forgiveness. To progress,"

On the stage I saw Abigail and Kaitlin, arm in arm, smiling. The two former roommates, friends again. Kaitlin had changed her look. Gone were the dreadlocks. In were the bangs. Abigail looked slightly older, less innocent, but wiser. Full of strength.

"Well, Pasch, you wanna head down there?"

"We better not." He nodded. He knew what I meant. Going down there would just remind them all of the bad times from six months ago. They had all come so far since then. They had a lot to celebrate and we left them to it.

We walked back to the car. Walton still limping from that kick to Ike's knee. His body was still recovering from that epic fight. I think he had been sleeping in bathtubs full of ice. The Grateful Dead started playing from Bill's portable Bluetooth speaker. Jerry Garcia was singing about the reasons he cries away each lonely night. The first one was sweet Anne Marie. She was his heart's delight.

"Where to next, Bill?"

"Hawaii, Dave," Walton said. "You know that. Maui Invitational. Best week of the year. I love Maui. I've got some great old friends who live down there."

"Yeah, I know, Bill. But I meant more in the grander sense. Where do we go now?"

"Dave, let's set out running, but let's take our time."

We walked back to the production van, where Stephanie waited. She was not alone. The Colonel sat by her side.

"Aloha, Walton!"

"Stephanie, are you taking your whole family? This is a work trip."

"No, Ana is safe and sound with my mom. Stephanie will be busy with you two," said the Colonel. "And I plan to hit all four military golf courses in Hawaii while I'm there. You golf, Walton?"

"Heavens, no. Too violent a sport for me."

"Okay, gotta go. I can't wait to get to Hawaii!" Nick ran up, excitedly showing us the Air Jordans he wore for the occasion. They were artfully festooned with plumeria and hibiscus flowers along with Polynesian tribal designs. I still had on my plain old hiking boots. I had become rather attached to them. Nick hopped behind the wheel. He was driving us to the airport, hopefully slower than our last trip together. Walton and I got in the van and we were off to the airport and then westward towards the setting sun and the land of rainbows.

Aloha.

Kia Ora.

The Bill Walton Mysteries
will continue in Hawaii...

ABOUT THE AUTHOR

James Kirkland was born in Portland, Oregon and attended Grant High School. He studied writing at Emerson College. Afterwards he worked as a comedian and improviser at Boom Chicago in Amsterdam. He now lives in Los Angeles. This is his first novel. James also has a graphic novel he self-published called *Kaiju vs Jaeger: A Love Story*. James is a diehard fan of the Portland Trailblazers and still thinks Greg Oden was the right decision.

Made in the USA
Las Vegas, NV
22 February 2021